# Out of Darkness

## Darrell Case

Proverbs 11:30
**Leaning Tree Christian Publishers**
Post Office Box 6124
Terre Haute, IN 47802

# Out of Darkness

**Out of Darkness**

Copyright © 2012 by Darrell Case

Printed in the United States of America
ISBN: 9780615601861

Learn more information at:
www.darrellcase.com

To my loving wife Connie.
I could not have done it without you.

Presented to:

From:

Date:

# Contents

# ACKNOWLEDGMENTS

As I said in *Live Life to the Fullest*, no one who writes a book does it alone. There are those whose names do not appear on the cover but should. My thanks to Justin Davis for the cover design. My editor Mary Ellen Robertson. To those who believed in this author and encourage him to keep on going when he wanted to quit. My chief encourager is my wife Connie, then my church family and of course The Lord Jesus Christ. To these I say thank you. The book is completed lets pray God uses it for His glory.

# Chapter 1

David Padgett's success haunted him. A deep-seated fear gripped his heart. He felt as if he were teetering on the edge of a bottomless chasm. One step in the wrong direction and he would plunge into a darkness so deep he could never return. A sense of loneliness and despair besieged him.

Last night Jeff Berry had phoned from New York. "I gotta tell you, David, I've been your agent for a long time. This book? It's your best yet. Are you ready for this? The publisher's sales arm has sold fifty thousand advance copies of *Love Unlimited*." David smiled at the news and Jeff's breathless conveyance of it. "You mark my words, you're headed for the best seller list again."

This morning David sighed, rose from his antique desk and circled his office aimlessly. The opulent golden oak wainscoting gleamed under the crystal Art Deco chandelier, reflecting the rich leather couch and chairs. Luxurious as they were, his surroundings held no pleasure for him. Even the lofty strains of Beethoven struck his ears discordantly. He turned off the Bose.

His eyes drifted across the photos and commendations from Ronald Reagan, Jimmy Carter, Bill Clinton, Pope John Paul and other persons of note that lined the walls, along with honorary doctorates from several Christian Collages. Always before their words of praise had cheered and inspired him. He turned to gaze through the full glass that comprised both exterior walls of his office. His ghostly reflection stared back at him. His heart felt cold and indifferent to the plight of the world.

At 50, plastic surgery and a pricey colorist gave him the appearance of a man in his late 30s. Only the graying hair at his temples betrayed him. The PR Department insisted he leave the touch of silver, saying it gave him an air of distinction. Studying his image in the glass, he smoothed his hair and stood ramrod straight as he brushed a speck of imaginary dust from his Kiton suit. He straightened his silk Jacquard tie. Then he relaxed and let his shoulders slump. There were no cameras around, at least he hoped not.

David's third-story office afforded him a sweeping view of Grace Tabernacle's 150-acre estate, the tranquil village of Grafton and the White River meandering in the distance. He watched as an exquisite red June sunrise ushered in a perfect late spring day. A light mist rose lazily from the river. Dew on the grass sparkled like a billion gems. "My acres of diamonds," David whispered, "are filled with fool's gold."

He returned to the desk and opened his scheduling book. The day was full of meetings and promotional filming. Global Outreach currently reached 80 countries via broadband internet. Podcasting his sermons and promoting his books, the website generated thousands of hits a day. The order department was kept constantly busy shipping his books, CDs and sermon notes.

David slammed the book closed. When was the last time he and Anne were able to take a vacation? Not a four-day trip with a speaking engagement sandwiched in, but some time together away from everything. He was the envy of every minister in the world, yet he would trade places with the pastor of a small country church in a heartbeat.

Shoving back his chair, David jumped to his feet and went to the far side of the office. The floor-to-ceiling bookcase concealed the door to David's secret room. He, Anne and Robert were the only ones privy to it.

Searching the shelves, he pulled out a signed copy of Rick Warren's *The Purpose Driven Life.* Among the more than 1,000 books he owned, many of them autographed, this book held a special place in his heart. He breathed in the smell of the custom leather as he ran his fingers over the cover. David loved the smell of fine leather.

As in his high school years, he could still lose himself in a good book. It was easier for him to be mesmerized by the characters in a novel than to deal with real people in real life.

2

Today, however, neither the rows of best sellers nor his tony office afforded him a scintilla of joy.

"Tell me, Rick, didn't you ever want to just walk away?" he murmured. He thought about calling the author but quickly rejected the idea.

Except for the foundation and electrical work, David built the original Grace Tabernacle virtually singlehandedly. As such, it was a painfully primitive structure. He spent two years trying to convince the Grafton city leaders that the church was an asset, not an eyesore. Grafton's oak-lined streets, stately homes and manicured lawns were right out of the pages of *Ideal* magazine. The crime rate in Grafton was among the lowest in the state, in great contrast to Indianapolis. Mothers felt safe letting their children go off alone to play in the park with their friends. At night, couples still ventured out to stroll unafraid hand-in-hand along the streets.

Resisting encroachment by Walmart and other big chains, the residents cherished their downtown. Individuals, not corporations, owned the pharmacy, hardware, and grocery stores. On Friday and Saturday nights, the old Grand Theater did a thriving business. The Grafton High Lions boasted three state championships in the last 10 years. Bucking the popular trend, Grafton's business district was closed on Sundays. The store owners joked it would be pointless to open as everyone, including them, would be attending services at Grace Tabernacle. David had hoped the jest would someday be fact.

The small, white clapboard church building at the far end of the property seemed desolate now and woefully out of place. Starkly unadorned, it stood in mean contrast to its opulent surroundings. Several narrow walking paths led to the building's entrance and side doors. Their half-buried, faded gray slate stepping stones did nothing to enhance the tiny house of worship's appeal.

David pictured the hand-carved and lettered wooden plaque beside the front door:

*Grace Tabernacle, built by the two hands*

*of our beloved pastor, Dr. David Padgett.*

*From his humble beginnings*

*he built a worldwide ministry.*

—Donated by Youth Aglow

The inside of the building was numbingly plain. The rough-hewn wooden pews were bought at auction from an abandoned Methodist church. The boxy pulpit was inelegantly fashioned out of plywood. The two-man maintenance crew touched up the exterior paint every spring and did what they could to repair any damage caused by age or weather. As more property was acquired and buildings sprang up to accommodate the growing congregation, David wondered if the small church building should be demolished. The members protested, saying they wanted to preserve Grace Tabernacle's beginning.

Thinking back, David smiled remembering how happy he and Anne had been then. Their first Christmas in Grafton, the young parents had limited themselves to exchanging only cards so Bobby could have a real Christmas. The following spring David spent the last of his inheritance to lay the foundation of the church. He took a job as a sacker at John's Super Value. Anne stood behind his decision, working three days a week at the Hair Place Beauty Shop.

David shivered thinking of the endless hours he had spent combing the streets for building fund donations. Each morning at 8:30 he was out of the house and knocking on doors. Braving the worst blizzard in 20 years, he made five calls before frostbite threatened. All that winter into the spring and summer, he kept knocking until he had visited every home and business in Grafton and the surrounding countryside.

Winding up his rounds at 11:45, he would rush home for

4

a quick bite and to rest awhile. At 2 PM, he'd be sacking groceries at the Super Value, then back home by nine. Exhausted, he would spend an hour with Anne and drop into bed to start all over again the next day.

On the church's inaugural Sunday morning, he arrived at 9:15 to welcome his congregation. That first Lord's Day, and every Sunday for 45 weeks thereafter, he preached to a congregation of two. Anne would smile and nod her head each time he made a point. Their only distraction was Bobby, who squirmed in the pew while his mother tried in vain to keep him still.

On more Monday mornings than he could count, David quit the ministry. Before the end of the week, Anne would persuade him to try one more time. On the 46th Sunday, halfway through the service, in walked Ed Harden and his wife, Ada. David stopped in mid-sentence and stepped down from the pulpit to welcome them.

"Sorry for being late, Preacher," Ed said, "but the hogs got out just as we was a-leavin." David nodded and shook Ed and Ada's hands enthusiastically. Stepping back to the pulpit, he started the sermon from the beginning. Ten years later, Ed sold his hog farm to become head groundskeeper of the new Grace Tabernacle.

Today, the trappings of 25-year-old Robert's office rivaled those of his father's. As Executive Associate Pastor, the young preacher formerly known as Bobby was poised to take over when David retired or died.

Seven days a week, Global Outreach carried David's messages throughout the world. Every Sunday three shifts of attendants ushered 2,000 people in and out of the cavernous sanctuary. Three services, the first at 8:00 the last at 11:30, wore him out. By the end of the day, David could repeat his sermon in his sleep. Anne complained he often did. Week after week, letters and emails poured in from every corner of the globe. All correspondence was read and answered by a response team secluded in a small back room. David rarely saw any of it.

5

Preacher David was a prolific author. Time after time his books topped the New York Times Best Seller List, making his name a household word. His publisher offered his latest book signed and gift-boxed for $100. Sales skyrocketed. David had to be content with the promotional aspect; his cut was nominal.

Every day, calls from ministries and corporations flooded the receptionist's desk. Jenny Macklin ran her station like a battleship's bridge. She knew how to handle small ministries, start-up companies and anyone else lacking deep pockets. She did so with a perpetual smile in her voice.

"Preacher David's fee is forty thousand a day plus expenses. Please hold, I'll connect you with our finance department. They will discuss payment arrangements and his schedule with you." If there was a mumbled response about having to call back, Jenny would hit the disconnect button like a general launching a nuclear strike.

"Didn't think so." Without missing a beat, she would punch the button for the next caller. "Grace Tabernacle, how may I help you?" Her pleasant voice held an approachable southern twang and her friendly greeting made each caller feel like the most important person in the world. Sometimes David would stand near her desk listening and marvel at her proficiency.

Twelve months a year, David crisscrossed the country giving seminars. His spiritually oriented, path-to-success presentations were highly in demand. Attendees were mainly ladder-climbers from Fortune 500 companies willing and able to pay hundreds for the privilege. At each seminar, security turned away pastors from small churches. Relying on Preacher David's largesse, they came hoping to be allowed in despite not being able to pay the entire fee, or at all. At the last meeting, held at a Hilton, a man broke through the barriers and raced toward the convention hall. A security officer took off after him and grabbed him from behind. David watched from a balcony as the guard muscled the pastor out through the glass doors.

6

"Please let me in. I just want to learn how to reach more people for Christ." His pleas fell on deaf ears and the seminar went on without him. That man reminded David of himself 20 years ago. He sighed. For all he had accomplished, the happiness he preached to thousands of others evaded him.

At one time, David Padgett considered himself the most fortunate man in the world. Graduating from Taylor University, he arrived in Grafton with a small inheritance from his mother's estate and an outsized dream. After a week of searching, he found a dilapidated house on 25 acres at the edge of town, not yet country, but far enough away from the city. He managed to purchase the property on a land contract. He worked on the shack for weeks, sometimes with little sleep. After two months, the house was livable. He brought Anne and Bobby to Grafton and began building the church. For months, he poured his labor into the building at night, visited house-to-house each morning and worked at the Super Value afternoons and evenings. Then his life changed, forever.

Tired but restless after his shift at the Super Value, David walked to the framed-out church. Staring at the bare two-by-fours in the tiny Sunday school room, he picked up his hammer. A small voice spoke inside him. "It'll never happen. Ten years from now you'll still be at the Super Value all day and banging nails all night, for nothing."

With hopelessness weighing on his heart, he dropped the hammer and crossed the overgrown field to his home. Entering the living room, he sank into the easy chair he had rescued from the dump. The smell of the apple pie Anne just took out of the oven wafted through the house. She didn't say a word, just brought him a cup of coffee, a piece of pie and the *Indianapolis Star*.

Flipping through the paper, he saw the answer to his prayer. Practically jumping off the page was a half-page ad for a business seminar with billionaire Tibb Russell that Saturday at the Holiday Inn. Russell had clenched and clawed his way up from poverty as a wunderkind in stocks, bonds and insurance. The seminar fee was $200 in advance, $250 at the door. David calculated their savings. He could make it, barely.

Calling Anne in from the kitchen, David said, "Look at this." She peered over his shoulder. He tapped the ad with his finger. "This is just what I need."

"Yes, it looks good. But dear," she said, resting her chin on his shoulder, "you're a pastor, not a salesman."

"I am a salesman, Anne. My product is the best remedy known to man, the gospel of Jesus Christ."

Unconvinced, Anne said, "Honey, I don't think this is right. But if you do, I'll help you all I can."

"I love you," David said. Pushing himself up from the sagging cushion, he took her in his arms and kissed her. "I'm sure this is just what I need to build a healthy, vital church."

At eight o'clock Saturday morning, David stood in a line extending all the way down the hall from the Holiday Inn's ballroom. Snippets of conversations among the professionally dressed men and women in front of and behind him drifted within earshot. They were discussing difficult customers, sales figures and stifling government regulations. David felt like a fish out of water. The line moved at a snail's pace toward the registration table until it was finally his turn. An attractive blonde woman in a royal blue suit took a form from the stack.

"Name please?" she said without looking up.

"Rev..., uh, David Padgett," he said, thinking quickly. He wasn't sure he wanted it known that he was a minister.

"Company name?" she asked, smiling but clearly in a hurry to move things along. He hesitated. All of these men and women were here for one reason only: to increase their sales. He wanted to learn how to lead more souls to Christ. Her smile faded. "It's perfectly acceptable if you don't want the name of your business to appear on your tag. However, I am required to list it for our records."

David's cheeks burned. He leaned over the table and whispered, "Grace Tabernacle."

"Excuse me?" she said, knitting her eyebrows.

"Grace Tabernacle church," he said a little louder.

Handing him a blank name tag, she said rather briskly, "Have a nice day."

# Chapter 2

Seated unobtrusively at the far end of the back row, David used his ink pen to write his name on the sticky tag. He noticed others had written theirs in black magic marker. For the next two-and-a-half hours, he wrote furiously on the back of the program notes, taking down everything Tibb Russell said. The man was a dynamic individual, an eccentric genius and proud of it. He easily held the attention of what looked to David like hardened, no-nonsense executives.

One minute they were roaring with laughter, the next their eyes filled with tears as Tibb related one of his heart-rending, life-changing stories. As the time flew by, David had a vision of himself preaching from a magnificently ornate pulpit with thousands of people falling at his feet. At the conclusion of the seminar, he ran from the building, his heart racing. He couldn't wait to put Tibb's principles into practice.

Sitting in the tiny square that would be his church office, David sat under a bare light bulb and went day into night rewriting and perfecting his notes. Finally at 2 AM, he crept into his and Anne's bedroom, expecting her to be asleep. "Can you use what you learned today, sweetheart?" Anne asked, propping herself up on an elbow to look at him.

Lying back on his pillow, David covered his eyes with his forearm. "Yes, most of it is good information, useful information, but there are some points I wish I could clarify."

"Could you meet with this man one on one?" she asked, rolling into David's arms.

"Honey, do you have any idea what Tibb Russell charges for a private consultation? Seven hundred and fifty dollars, and that's just for the first half hour," David said, sighing. "I cleaned out our savings just for today."

"I could sell my piano," she offered.

"No, honey. I couldn't ask you to do that," David said, kissing his wife on the forehead.

"No, really. I can still use the one at the church." The darkness hid her tears.

"That old thing? It's so far out of tune it's in the next county." Anne's laughter always sounded to David like wind chimes. "Besides, you love that Steinway."

"Yes, but I love you more. And besides, when you build a big, fine church you'll buy me a new one.'

He took Anne at her word. The next morning he placed an ad in the Grafton Gazette. Three calls came in before the ink was dry. Using some of the techniques he learned from Tibb Russell, David negotiated a bid higher than his asking price and sold the Steinway to the last caller. Anne concealed her tears behind a dishcloth as she watched her mother's wedding gift being loaded into the back of an old pickup truck.

Before heading to work, David called Russell's secretary. To his amazement, she had an opening that evening. Yes, he could make that. He smiled remembering how nervous he'd been entering Tibb's sphere just a couple of days ago.

Slogging through his shift at the Super Value, David was finding it difficult to focus his cerebral energy on the fine art of grocery bagging. He was putting Mrs. Mellon's sack in the back seat of her car when he heard her cane tap-tapping sharply on the asphalt behind him. "You've got the wrong car there, sonny," she said, her wrinkled face frowning at him. "Rough day today?" With a mumbled apology, he quickly pulled out the sack and followed her to her car. He set the groceries down lightly on the front seat as she pointed to the designated spot with her wobbling cane. She drove away, no thank you, no tip.

David hurried home, showered, shaved and dressed in his best suit. Jumping into his dilapidated Chevy, he sped toward Indianapolis. His nervousness increased as he walked to the towering building. On the 15th floor, he located Tibb's office at the far end of the hall and slowly opened the door. Sitting behind a desk in the reception area was the blonde woman whose feathers he had ruffled at the registration table.

11

She greeted him with a smirk. "May I help you?" she asked in an icy tone.

"I... I have an appointment with Mr. Russell."

Looking disgruntled, she opened a leather bound book and ran her finger down the page. Turning her back to David, she lifted the phone, spoke into it briefly and replaced the handset. "You may go in. Mr. Russell is expecting you." She swiveled around in her chair and began clicking away on her keyboard.

Entering the mogul's office, David rubbed his sweat-soaked palms on his pants and hoped Tibb wouldn't notice. Motioning him to a chair, Russell scrutinized him from head to toe, his eyes boring into the young pastor. He let David squirm for a moment or two, then said, "What do you want?"

David's teeth fairly chattered. "I... er... that is... I... waa... want to increase my congregation."

"How many?"

"I... er... don't know. A bunch."

"And this bunch, what are their names?" David began listing the names of his congregants. His face burned at the feeble number.

"No, no, no!" Russell bellowed with exasperation. "Not those attending now, I'm talking about your future congregation. What are their names, how old are they? Are they single? Married? If so, how long have they been married and how many children do they have? What are their children's names? How old are they? What percentage should be men, women, children? "

"Whoa, excuse me," David said, rising from the chair in anticipation of being thrown out. "I haven't even met my future congregation. How would I know their names?"

Russell stood and leaned across the desk. "You will never see a bunch of people coming into your church until you see them in your mind's eye."

"Okay," David said dubiously, nervously retaking his seat.

"And when, if, you get this bunch of people, what happens when you run out of room?"

"I... I guess I'll build on."

"So you're a contractor? I thought you said you're a minister," Russell goaded, dropping back into his chair.

"I am sir, but I don't have the money to hire someone," David said, lowering his eyes.

"And why don't you?" Russell asked brusquely.

"Because we don't have enough people and the ones we do have are poor."

"Exactly!" Tibb Russell yelled, pointing his finger at David. "Now, Reverend, without even knowing it you're getting the point of our discussion. The people attending your church are hamstrung by insufficient income. Oh, I'm sure they're good people, salt of the earth and all that. However, you'll never build a large church on an empty pocketbook."

"Well, what can I do?" David asked, his heart sinking.

"What you need, my friend, is a marketing plan."

"Marketing plan? I'm sorry, I don't understand."

"What is it people want, what is it they need?

"I'm not sure," David mumbled. He wondered why he had ever thought an unsaved businessman could help him boost his church attendance. "I know they need salvation."

"All right," Russell said, linking his hands behind his head. "This salvation, you think it's important in people's lives?"

"It is the most important aspect in their lives and for the well-being of our nation."

"So you believe it will change their lives, make them better people?"

"I know it will," David said, gearing up to defend his faith.

"Oh, come on, Reverend!" Russell yawped as he brought his hand down on his desk with a bang. He paused to catch his breath. His tone softened a little, but remained intimidating. "Be realistic, young man. You mean to tell me you think reading a few Bible verses and praying a little prayer is going to make an alcoholic sober, a drug addict clean, a prostitute forsake that vile life?" Shaking his head, Russell sniggered derisively.

David jumped up, his face red, his fists clenched. "Yes, that's exactly what I'm telling you. I've seen it happen." Heading for the door, he turned and faced a surprised Tibb Russell. Close to tears, David summed up their meeting. "Obviously, I've come to the wrong place for advice. I thought you could help me."

"Sit down, Reverend," Russell said softly. "I can help you."

The change in the atmosphere was so sudden and compelling that David returned meekly to his seat. "Can you really help me?"

"Yes, my friend, I can. However, my formula will only work if you follow it to the letter."

"But you just denigrated everything I believe in."

"No, what I did was ignite the passion you have hidden within. David, whether you want to sell insurance or Jesus Christ, you must first believe passionately in your product. You must believe it's the greatest, the most needed, invention since the wheel." Russell got up and faced the large window overlooking the White River. "All right, make a believer out of me," he said. He turned, leaned against the window sill and folded his arms across his chest. "You have five minutes."

David panicked. He felt lost without his Bible. His mind was spinning with random salvation verses. The clock was ticking. After a minute he settled down enough to start his presentation. The preacher who delivered his sermons with smooth confidence Sunday after Sunday now stammered, hesitated, and bumbled. He was only halfway through when Russell raised his hand.

"Time," he announced like a coach with a stopwatch. Falling into his chair, David hung his head. "Wonderful," Russell said, beaming.

"What?" David said, expecting to be ridiculed again.

"I could feel your passion. You certainly believe

14

in what you're selling."

"But I made a mess of it. The gospel is a beautiful, wonderful message."

"True, your presentation was atrocious."

Stinging with humiliation, David muttered, "What can I do?"

"Repackage it."

"What's that?"

"Here, let me give you an illustration." Seating himself, Tibb took a box of Cracker Jacks from his desk drawer, opened it and thrust in two fingers. As he pulled them out, David saw a ring between his thumb and forefinger. "Tell me, Reverend, how much is this worth?" He held it out for David's inspection.

David took a quick glance. "Oh, a few cents, maybe a nickel at most."

"Uh huh." Russell appeared to place it back in the box. Reaching into the drawer a second time, he set a small blue jeweler's box on the desk and opened it. Embossed in gold script on the satin lining above the sparkling ring was the word Tiffany's. "Now, how much is this one worth?"

"May I get a closer look?"

"By all means," Russell said, pushing the box across to him.

David picked up the box. As he did, the diamonds caught the sunlight. "Now this is a real gem," he said, studying it admiringly. "This must be worth five or six thousand dollars."

"Wrong, David," Russell said, smiling. "This ring is valued at over twenty-two thousand. It's the same one I took out of the Cracker Jacks box." David's jaw dropped. He set the box back on the desk.

"Packaging is everything." Tibb said, placing the ring back in the drawer.

"So you're saying I should package the gospel differently?"

"Exactly!" Russell exclaimed. "It doesn't change the message, just the vehicle."

15

"How would you suggest I do that?" David asked. He leaned forward, eager to hear.

"Take a survey of the general population of your town and the surrounding areas," Russell said, writing on a sheet of paper. "Find out what the people want and give it to them. Of course, you may have to modify your product."

David looked uneasy. "What do you mean, modify?"

"If I discover one of my policies isn't selling, I find out why. If I have to reword it, I will. If I need to change the coverage, I do."

"You're saying I should change my method of preaching?"

"Absolutely. Fire and brimstone preaching is a thing of the past. Today, people are running to psychologists and counselors. If you want to help your people, give them therapeutic preaching."

David was lost, and very skeptical. "Therapeutic preaching?"

"Certainly," Russell said, his face beaming. "Deliver messages relevant to their everyday lives. People today want to improve their marriages, learn the best method of child rearing and how to succeed in their profession. Why, sometimes even throw in a sermon about the family dog."

"You are kidding."

"Reverend, people pay billions of dollars to lie on therapists' and psychologists' couches. Why not have some of that money come your way and help people at the same time?"

"Do you really think I can build a large church?"

"Do you?" Russell asked.

"I, I guess so, I don't know."

"Are you employed, Reverend?"

David's face reddened. "Yes, I sack groceries at John's Super Value."

Russell let David linger in his embarrassment for a moment before saying, "No offense, but folks don't want the kid who bags their groceries on Saturday telling them how to live on Sunday."

16

"You think I should change jobs?"

"No, I think you should be a full-time preacher."

"I have a wife and son. How will we live?"

Tibb reached into the desk drawer and pulled out his checkbook. "About once a year I bankroll someone who I believe has great potential for success in their chosen field." He handed David a list of books. "Go to your local bookstore and buy these." *Think and Grow Rich* was the only one David recognized. "Follow their instructions to the letter."

"They seem to be all about business," David said as his eyes wandered from the list to the checkbook. He didn't dare ask Russell what bankrolling him would entail. Tibb leaned back in his chair, stretched and linked his fingers behind his head.

"Reverend, would you say I'm successful?"

"Of course, very!" David exclaimed, glancing around the richly appointed office.

"The practice I'm going to share with you has made me one of the wealthiest men in the United States. Every evening I spend one hour in a darkened room. I allow no interruptions. After emptying my mind of anything troubling me, I have my advisors come in for a meeting."

"Every night? I'm not sure my two deacons could come every night."

"You misunderstand, sir," Russell said, smiling. "The advisors I speak of are able to attend any meeting, day or night. Close your eyes." David did so. "Now," Russell said, his voice soft and low, "think of your wife. Do you have a picture of her in your mind?"

"Yes."

"Let her speak to you." Russell waited. David smiled. "What is she saying?" Opening his eyes, David blushed. Tibb roared, his laughter bouncing off the walls. "Never mind, Reverend. The principle you just used is how I have board meetings in my dark room. This way you can meet with any leader, living or dead, at any time.

"Reverend, I'm going to loan you one hundred thousand dollars for the next five years, interest free."

David jumped to his feet. "No, sir, I couldn't accept that. I mean I appreciate it and all but—"

"Reverend, just as no father wants his daughter to marry a grocery store sacker, nobody you'd want sitting in your church wants him as their pastor. What I'm offering you is not charity, but a chance to fulfill your dreams."

David hesitated.

"If you're not interested, I'll extend the opportunity to the next young man waiting to see me. Well?"

"I'll do it!"

# Chapter 3

David finished sketching the building and grounds designs one month after meeting with Tibb Russell. When he showed them to Anne, she gasped and her hand flew up to her heart. "Fifteen millionaires is all it would take to finance it," David said excitedly.

Built in the shape of a cross, Grace Tabernacle was an architect's dream. The glassed-in vestibule boasted a stunning rose garden with special lighting to coax buds into richly-hued blooms 12 months a year. Water from a three-tiered fountain cascaded into a koi pond in the center of the garden. Marble benches surrounding it invited visitors to rest and contemplate their direction in life.

Luxuriously furnished men's and women's lounges leading into marble and brass restrooms flanked the entranceway. At a long counter situated between the two huge sets of sanctuary doors, smiling staff members stood ready to help visitors and members alike. Scripted in gold on the wall behind them were the words:

*Every possibility a dream*

*Every dream a possibility*

*For with God nothing shall be impossible.*

Shops lined both wings of the cross. On the west side were a Starbucks, McDonald's and The Upper Room, an upscale restaurant. The opposite wing offered Kay Jewelers, The Beautiful You beauty salon, an Old Navy store and The Cross Christian book store. Hidden speakers transmitted classical music throughout the first floor, with the exception of the auditorium.

Enormous stained glass windows shaped like crosses lined the walls of the sanctuary. Each depicted a Bible theme:

19

Moses crossing the Red Sea, Christ praying in the garden, Christ ascending into Heaven. It was David's decision to omit Christ dying on the cross.

The huge platform with its state-of-the art sound and lighting systems rivaled a Hollywood studio. Tiers of plush upholstered seats made the sanctuary appear more like a Broadway theater. A 200-voice choir accompanied by a 50-piece orchestra opened each service. Twenty spacious Sunday school rooms took up the second floor, some with a capacity of 200. Still, most Sundays many would be turned away for lack of seating. The church offices occupied the third floor.

At the foot of the cross-shaped structure, David's office overlooked Eden Park. The centerpiece of the sprawling park was an arched, white stone footbridge spanning the teardrop-shaped lake that tapered into a placid lily pond. In the middle of the lake, a fountain sprayed a fan of water 30 feet into the air. At night, a circle of lights gave the spray a golden hue. Walking paths wound through dense stands of lavish ornamental trees. Antique gas lamps at 50-foot intervals illuminated the walkways with soft yellow light.

Formal gardens thick with color graced the entire length of the lake's north side. Alabaster statues of such Christian leaders as Moody, Spurgeon, Billy Sunday and others stood regally among the vivid blooms. Granite benches were strategically spaced so the faithful could enjoy the gardens with a measure of privacy. A shady picnic area was situated at the edge of the lily pond. Just east of the lake, a 12,000-seat amphitheater was built into the hillside in a masterfully innovative stroke of construction and acoustical engineering.

On the east side of the property, David and Anne's plantation-style mansion rose above a five-and-a-half foot tall hedgerow. To discourage prying eyes, a five-foot high stone wall lined with towering poplars encircled their back lawn and infinity pool. Two hundred yards to the west, an identical mansion housed Robert and May.

From his office window, David watched as a young couple paused on the arch of the footbridge. He smiled. Many a young man had knelt there to propose to his beloved. Perhaps these two would be married in the formal garden. He was sure they were members of his church. An eight-foot high chain link fence skirting its perimeter, along with round-the-clock security patrols, ensured the park was exclusive to members of Grace Tabernacle. David knew that more than one family had joined the church primarily to gain access to the park. He couldn't remember the last time he and Anne had walked the garden paths. Thinking of their lost love left him with a hollow feeling in the pit of his stomach.

On the bridge, the couple seemed to be embroiled in an argument. The woman laid her hand on the man's arm. He jerked away. She tried again. He walked to the end of the bridge. She followed. Whirling on her, he pounded his fist on the railing.

David always steered clear of spying on people in the park. He was aware that some couples used it as a lovers' lane. Some of the elderly members had complained about it. David considered it none of his business. As their shepherd, his job was to lead by example, not ride herd over the flock. But this seemed serious. He reached into his bottom desk drawer for the binoculars Anne gave him last Christmas for bird watching.

"Better keep an eye on them," he murmured. "If he gets violent, I'll call security." He adjusted the focusing wheels and zeroed in on the man. A tremor ran through him as he watched his son pounding the rail and screaming at the woman. A vein throbbed in Robert's flushed forehead.

David moved his vision field slightly to the left. Ellen Ridgeway, a 24-year-old production assistant, burst into tears and ran across the bridge to the church. A minute later Robert followed, entering the building through a side door.

A stab of fear ripped through David's heart. Something was dreadfully wrong. Maybe he should speak to Robert. What would he say? He remembered Robert was holding a marriage seminar this weekend at the lake. David buzzed

Mattie Jeffers, Robert's secretary. "Mattie, when Robert comes in please tell him I'd like to see him."

"Yes, sir," Mattie said. "I'm not sure when he'll be... Oh, he just came in, Pastor. I'll tell him right now."

"Thank you." David laid the binoculars back in the drawer and covered them with a sheaf of papers. A few minutes later there was a soft knock at the door.
"Come in," David called, struggling to keep his voice steady.

Stepping into the room, Robert closed the door and stood before it like a soldier at attention, clenching and unclenching his fists. His stance and expression were identical to those he had displayed at the age of five when he was caught stealing a small toy from the five and dime. David noticed the knuckles of his right hand were bloody.

"Come in son," David said. "Have a seat." Robert sat stiffly on the edge of the couch. "Would you like a soda?"

"No thanks, Dad," Robert said, holding his blood-smeared hand beside his right thigh, out of David's view.

David sat down on Robert's left. "I wanted to ask you about the couples' gathering this weekend. Have all the speakers confirmed?"

"Yes," Robert said, letting out his breath.

"Are there any issues we need to address?"

Robert turned toward his father. His mouth opened but he hesitated, then said, "Uh, no, everything's on track."

"I thought your mother and I might attend," David said, staring at the glass of Coke in his hand.

"Checking up on me, Dad?" Robert's lips smiled, but his eyes did not.

"No, of course not, son," David said too quickly. He took a large gulp; the cold liquid cooled his flushed cheeks. "I just thought it would be nice to relax and listen to someone else speak for a change."

"Sorry," Robert said, letting down his guard. "I'd be delighted if you and Mom would come. But isn't Mom going to Atlanta?"

"Change of plans," David said simply, hoping Anne would agree to cancel her speaking engagement.

"Great." Robert got up to leave. "Then I'll see you both tomorrow morning. I have to go. I'm playing golf with the mayor this afternoon."

"That's right. I forgot. Be sure and let him win," David said with a chuckle.

"He always does," Robert said, smiling.

As soon as the door closed, David called Anne's secretary. "Mrs. Padgett's office. Jane Goodley speaking. May I help you?"

"Hello, Jane. Is she busy?"

"She's in a meeting with the ladies from Silver Lake. Would you like me to put you through?"

Anne often bragged that Jane was the best secretary in the church. She acted as a buffer between her boss and the world, only interrupting Anne's meetings for David or Robert.

"No, no, that's not necessary," David said. "Just tell her I'd like to see her when she's finished."

Ten minutes later Anne came in. She admired her husband's profile as he stood gazing through the glass wall. He looked so distinguished with just that tinge of gray at his temples. The scars from his most recent surgery were hidden behind his ears and under his hairline. His posture was perfect. Anne smiled thinking how different he was from the nervous young pastor of the tiny church.

"Ya'll wanna see me, boss?" she asked with the faux southern accent that always made him laugh.

"Sit down, Anne, I need to speak to you," David said. Anne felt a chill when she saw the stress lines creasing his face. They sat facing each other on the couch. "I told Robert we would be at the couples gathering this weekend."

"Oh, David, that's impossible," Anne protested, turning away from his gaze. "I'm slated as the keynote speaker at Women's Rejoice in Atlanta."

"This is important, Anne. I believe he's in trouble."

23

"Robert in trouble? No, surely not," Anne said. David recounted the incident on the bridge. "David, you're overreacting," she said, stepping to the window. "Are you sure it was him? From this distance you can't even make out facial features."

"I was looking through the binoculars," David said, rising to stand next to her.

"Then you must have misinterpreted their actions."

"No, Anne, if you saw their faces you would have drawn the same conclusion. I'm sure he was holding back from striking her."

"I can't believe that. I'm sorry, David, I'm committed to this engagement and I must go."

"Why are you so insistent about this one conference, Anne?" David prodded, dropping into his desk chair. "We've both had to cancel speaking engagements in the past."

Anne bit her lip. "Remember the brochure from the Mercedes dealership you saw on the coffee table?"

"Yes." David drew out the word, not liking what was coming.

"I signed an order for a Roadster. I pick it up on Monday," Anne said excitedly, clasping her hands together. "The honorarium will make a sizable down payment."

"Anne, I thought we agreed to not buy any more cars until the Newsweek fallout cools down."

"I know." She looked at him pleadingly. "But I'll be able to manage the payments with the fees I receive from this and more engagements coming up."

"And that means you'll be traveling more. Anne, we hardly spend any time together as it is."

"I'll only be gone once or twice a month." Anne hoped she sounded convincing. She wasn't well practiced at telling little white lies. She decided a bit of leverage might push him in her direction. "David, remember the Honda?"

"Oh yes. It used more oil than gas," he said, smiling as he pictured the beat-up rust bucket.

"And remember what you said?"

24

"Certainly. I said if Grace Tabernacle grew the way I knew it would, I would never put you in danger by letting you drive another jalopy. But that's not the case. We have two cars in excellent condition and access to the church's limo."

"Yes. But they're not mine. They're titled to the church." Her green eyes locked onto his. "Please, David, this means a lot to me."

There was a time when David's holding out a dandelion plucked from the yard would bring a tear to Anne's eye. Now an immense sadness overtook him. He felt as if they had become strangers. He forced a smile. "I'll tell Robert it was too late for you to cancel. Have a good time in Atlanta."

"Thank you dear," she said, kissing him on the cheek.

"By the way, what color is the Roadster?"

"Baby blue with white leather interior," Anne said, her eyes sparkling. "Maybe we can take a drive up to New England this fall."

"Sure, hon," David said absently as she closed the door behind her. How was he going to explain his misstep to Robert?

Anne fairly skipped down the hallway to her office. She had dreaded this confrontation with David for days. Now the Lord had taken care of it in the simplest way. Wasn't He wonderful? "I named it, now I've claimed it," she whispered to herself.

The first time Anne saw the Roadster at Allan Motors, she knew she must have it. The exotic, low-slung convertible seemed to beckon to her from the glass-enclosed showroom. That night she pictured herself behind the wheel. Every night for the next month she lay awake thinking about it while David slept beside her. She envisioned herself speeding down the interstate, whizzing past everything in her way. By the end of the second week, she could feel the wind in her hair and the warm sun on her back. She felt silly lifting her hand and waving to the darkness, but right then silly felt good.

The fantasy expanded. Soon, Anne was not just waving at friends and church members as she cruised around town, but receiving admiring and envious stares in response. She mouthed greetings to them over the roar of the Roadster's engine. One night she forgot herself and actually called out to Linda Darby. In the vision, Mrs. Darby's mouth dropped open in surprise and envy.

The grumpy old widow was a thorn in Anne's side. She was worth more than fifty million and believed she ruled the church. The nasty old crone was always sending notes to David, complaining about his messages. Before each board meeting, she would write to the deacons demanding that David's salary be reduced. The board never even acknowledged, let alone acted upon, her letters and it infuriated her.

Pressing her foot on the accelerator, Anne laughed at the flummoxed old woman and sped away. David woke to her giggling with a start. Quickly she closed her eyes.

"Anne, are you all right?"

"Yes, dear," she murmured. "Sorry, I must have been dreaming." She was more careful after that. No need to fantasize about the Roadster. Monday it would be hers.,

# Chapter 4

Friday night David was greeted by an empty house. He always gave Helen, their cook, and Sarah, the housekeeper, weekends off to be with their families. He felt a pang of envy. There was a time when he and Anne spent every weekend together. Sometimes they did nothing more than enjoy each other's company at home. Or they would plan an evening in Indianapolis with dinner at the Eagle's Nest and then the symphony. Even when Robert was in high school and David began to travel, he made sure he was home by Friday night.

When had they lost that togetherness? He couldn't put his finger on a particular date, they had just gradually drifted apart over the years. Two years ago, complaining of David's restless tossing, Anne pushed for separate bedrooms. David was stunned and resisted as long as he could, but in the end he moved into the guest room at the end of the hall.

Last night Anne called to tell him of her safe arrival. David was working late in a production meeting. His voice mail took the call. If Anne followed her normal pattern, he wouldn't hear from her again until Sunday night. She would call a few minutes before her plane left Atlanta. When he first started traveling, they had burned up the phone lines. Sometimes they would talk for hours. There were months when their phone bill nearly matched what they spent on groceries. They discussed everything—struggles with the church, Robert, household problems, and of course, their love for each other.

After making a cold lunch meat sandwich around noon, David surfed the internet for hours, finally landing on a site describing the Women's Rejoice conference. He read Anne's bio chronicling her accomplishments in glowing terms. He felt both pride and a twinge of jealousy. Logging off, he was tempted to call her, but instead went to his bedroom and turned on the TV. He switched channels incessantly, finding nothing to hold his interest. Exhausted, he fell asleep with the lights on. After tossing and turning all night, he awoke Saturday morning as tired as if he hadn't slept a wink

After a quick shower, David dressed in jeans and a polo shirt. His breakfast consisted of three boiled eggs and a cup of instant coffee. "No use making a full pot," he muttered. The enormous house seemed to echo with loneliness.

David planned to wait until the seminar started at 10 and sneak in unnoticed. As he walked to the amphitheater, a late-coming couple spotted him. "Pastor! Hey, Pastor!" they shouted as they ran up to him. Others lingering in the park heard them and followed. He was quickly surrounded by a sizable crowd of admirers, many carrying copies of his latest book.

Open books, tracts, seminar programs, even an arm in a cast were thrust at him. With a smile bordering on a grimace, he signed each one. As the noisy group continued to mill around him, his eyes darted in the direction of the church. Where was security? Why didn't they rescue him? Finally after 10 minutes, a man in a blue uniform appeared. He looked to be barely out of his teenage years. "Okay, folks, time to go. The seminar started fifteen minutes ago, you're late," he said in a friendly but firm voice.

"Thank you, Officer... Crubble?" David said, glancing at the man's name tag.

"It's pronounced 'crooble', Pastor. Let me escort you over to the platform." As they walked side by side, David looked at the officer's profile. The thought struck him that possibly the young man wasn't saved. He put it out of his mind. Working at the church, Cruble and all the staff had countless opportunities to accept Christ. It wasn't David's responsibility to make certain they did.

Cruble wanted to make sure his boss didn't think him a slacker. "Sorry it took me so long to get here. Some of the neighborhood kids sneaked down to the lake with their fishing poles." David nodded. Once they reached the back door, Cruble left to continue his patrol.

On stage, the Christian rock band J.C. Freaks banged out their second number. David thought it sounded like a catfight in a hurricane. Oh well, he shouldn't criticize. The crowd was enjoying it. Swaying to the tune, they waved their hands in the air and sang along.

Backstage, Robert greeted his father and asked, "Where's Mom?"

"Glad to see you too, son," David answered mordantly.

"Sorry, Dad. One of the female speakers canceled. "Something about her child in the hospital. Can you believe that?"

"What about May? She does an excellent job with high school girls."

"Dad, this is a marriage seminar. What does May know about conflict in marriage?"

David's delivered his rejoinder with a biting laugh. "Well, she is married to you!" Robert stared at his father, a scowl creasing his forehead. "Relax, son! I was joking." The image of Robert and Ellen Ridgeway on the bridge flashed through David's mind.

"We'll make do," Robert said crossly.

To fill the dead spot in the program, Robert pressed his father into giving an informal talk on his latest book. Unprepared and nervous, David threw in a few marriage jokes, spicing them up to get an even bigger reaction. Raucous laughter bounced off the walls of the amphitheater and rolled across the lake into the surrounding neighborhood. Some laughed so hard they could barely breathe. A few of the older couples dropped their eyes, their cheeks flushing. As he returned to his seat in the back, David glanced at Robert and thought he saw resentment in his eyes.

After the gathering, David returned to the darkened house and found himself wondering about the choices he'd made in life. From all appearances, the marriage seminar was a huge success. At the invitation, 40 couples went forward to rededicate their commitment to each other. As he watched, David could not stop thinking, why are these people here? Is it because they want to be better Christians? Do they even know the Lord? From personal conversations with them, he knew several members of the Christian rock band were not believers. However, he would not interfere. They must make their own decisions.

After a simple meal of cold cuts, rye bread and potato salad, he showered and put on his pajamas. In the bedroom, he switched on the TV and flipped through the channels. He settled on a rerun of *Home Improvement*. After that show ended, *Little House on the Prairie* came on. As Pa held Caroline in his arms, David's thoughts drifted to Anne. Picking up the phone, he punched in the number for the Atlanta Hilton.

"I'm sorry sir, Mrs. Padgett hasn't returned. Would you care to leave a message?"

"No, I'll try again later. Thank you."

"Very good, sir. Have a nice night."

David thought about calling Anne's cell phone, but no. The last thing he needed was for her to think he was checking up on her.

# Chapter 5

In her one-bedroom cottage on the corner of Third and Grant streets, Ellen Ridgeway turned off the TV after watching the cartoon version of *Sleeping Beauty* for the third time. Ellen loved that movie. Each time she saw it she slipped into the role of Princess Aurora, with Robert as the handsome prince.

Last December Ellen had persuaded the head of the church's Elementary Department to perform the play for Parent's Day. It was a huge success, the thundering applause so protracted the production crew insisted that the blushing young director take a bow on stage. Afterward, Robert came backstage to congratulate her. He found her in the wardrobe room putting away the costumes.

Reacting with awkward excitement to the handsome pastor's presence, Ellen caught her foot between two boxes and stumbled. If Robert hadn't caught her, she would have tumbled face-first to the floor. As it was, she fell against his chest. Channeling her fairy tale heroine, Ellen raised her lips to Prince Charming. Closing her eyes, she envisioned the minister in shining armor. His lips were warm, almost feverish.

After that night, their liaison progressed with secret meetings where they would share each other's intimate ideas and dreams. Robert complained about his wife and the pressures of being David Padgett's son. Ellen assured him he was a wonderful speaker, as good as or better than his father. It all seemed so innocent, just two friends sharing the hardships of life. As meaningful glances edged their way into flirtatious teasing, double entendre soon came into play. Robert suggested they rendezvous at a motel 75 miles away.

"I'll be coming back from Cincinnati. We can meet at this Motel 6 just off the interstate. We'll have dinner together." It sounded so romantic. Ellen planned for days, agonizing over her closet's meager offerings of what to wear.

31

Frustrated, she bought a new dress, stretching her modest budget to the breaking point.

Sporting sunglasses and a wig, Ellen left Grafton. Ignoring her heart's convicting nudges, she checked into the motel under an assumed name. At 7 PM, Robert knocked on the door. She struggled to hide her disappointment as he stepped in holding a bag containing two Big Mac combo meals and a couple of Cokes.

Far from shaming eyes, their lovemaking began. Ellen shuddered at the memory. What she had thought would be so wonderful turned out to be the worst experience of her young life. In his haste, Robert essentially raped her. Her virginity gone along with her dignity, she lay under the covers muffling her sobs in the pillow. Oblivious, Robert sat in front of the TV wolfing down his sandwich and both orders of fries. When he finally realized she was upset, it took him half an hour to calm her down. By then her sandwich was cold. She took one bite and became nauseous. Dashing to the bathroom, she slammed the door in his face. Kneeling at the stool, she vomited. Some of it hit the seat and splashed onto her new dress. After cleaning up, she opened the door to a darkened room. Without a word, Robert was gone.

At the taping on Monday, she tried to catch his eye. He avoided her all week. Finally at noon on Friday in The Upper Room restaurant, she set her plate on the table and slid uninvited into the chair across from him.

Avoiding her eyes, Robert whispered, "Look, Ellen, I think it's best if we don't see each other again." He kept glancing around to make sure no one heard.

"But... but... you said you—" Ellen stuttered.

"Yes, Miss Ridgeway, I'll look into it," Robert said loudly as an elderly church member walked by, turning her head to look at them as she passed. "Thank you for bringing it to my attention."

Pushing back the chair with such force it nearly toppled over, Ellen left her food on the table and fled to the ladies room. Locking herself in a stall, she sat on the stool and sobbed in guilt and misery. After a few minutes, she dried her eyes, washed her face and touched up her makeup. She returned to her desk, determined to go on in spite of the pain in her heart.

As the weeks passed, she nearly succeeded. Then an odd sickness rudely interrupted her mornings. In sheer dread, she drove to the next town and bought a home pregnancy kit. The small cross confirmed her fears. Anticipation and despair hit her at the same minute. How she had dreamed of this day. So many times she had visualized herself sharing the wonderful news with her husband. Now that dream was shattered, and worse, so was her life.

Friday before work, Ellen waited for Robert in the church's west parking lot. He tried to sidestep her but she rushed ahead and stood in front of the door. Shushing her, he guided her to the bridge as she told him the news.

Robert could barely contain his anger. "How do you know it's mine?" he hissed.

"Robert, you're the only man I've ever been with," she cried, laying her hand on his arm as color rose in her face.

Yanking his arm away, he put his face inches from hers and snarled, "So you say. Listen, you try to pin this on me and I'll make you the laughing stock of this church and the whole town."

"People will believe me," Ellen said with more conviction than she felt.

"Sure they will," he said acerbically, his face twisting in rage. He pounded the bridge railing with his fist. "The daughter of the town drunk versus the son of one of the most famous preachers in the country!"

Taking a step back, Ellen stammered, "Robert, you know it's true. In your heart you know it is." Her eyes clouded with desperation. "Don't do this to me."

"It doesn't make any difference what I know. It's what people believe that's important. So go ahead, tell the whole world. All anyone will see is a pathetic little slut trying to railroad a man of God."

With her face burning and blinded by tears, Ellen ran to the church. Flying through the side door, she slowed to a fast walk past the receptionist. Ignoring the ringing phone, Jenny stood up and caught the distraught woman by the arm. "Ellen, are you all right?

Wiping her cheeks and clearing her throat, Ellen said huskily, "Yes. I just got some bad news."

"Is it your father? Is he in jail for drinking again? Is there anything I can do to help?" Grinning mischievously, Jenny ducked and weaved, putting up her hands in a mock defensive gesture. "Short of bailing him out, I mean?"

Ellen laughed a little. "No, it's not Dad." She threw her arms around Jenny. "You've been a good friend."

"Here comes Robert. Maybe he can help."

"No!" Ellen cried. Rushing down the hallway, she stopped short and turned to see Robert walking the other way. She went back to Jenny's desk. "There is one thing," she said softly.

"Name it."

"Pray for me?"

"Oo...kay," Jenny stammered, a question mark in her eyes.

"Thank you." Ellen proceeded down the hall to her office. Even as she disappeared into the production department, Jenny continued to stare after her.

"That girl's got problems. Pray for her. Yeah, right. Where's my to-do list?" Robert reappeared in the hallway. "Reverend Padgett," she called, lowering her voice as he approached. "Could you speak to Miss Ridgeway? She seems awfully upset."

"Yes, Jenny, thank you. I've already counseled and prayed with her in the garden."

Leaning over the desk, Jenny whispered, "Is it her father again?"

"Among other things," Robert whispered back. "Not a word of this to anyone, Jenny, please."

"Oh, of course." Conjuring her fake southern drawl, she picked up the phone. "Grace Tabernacle, how may I help you?" She promptly forgot about her encounters with Ellen and Robert.

After her co-workers left for the day, Ellen cleaned out her desk. With her hand on the light switch, she glanced around one last time. Her whole world for the last three years was contained in the shopping bag that dangled from her hand. After placing it in the trunk of her beat-up Escort, she took a small book off the front seat and re-entered the church. Walking to the other side of the building, she slipped through the back door of The Beautiful You.

Five years earlier, David had preached a sermon expounding on how women's spiritual joy enhances their outer beauty. The next day Esther Aldrich offered to relocate her beauty salon to the church's mall. The board of directors thought it was a wonderful idea. An upscale beauty salon seemed like the perfect complement to the ritzy promenade. The move proved to be profitable both for Esther and the church. With all the traffic from the staff, members and walk-ins, she had to hire two assistants.

"What can I do for you today, Ellen?" Esther asked. "Wash? Style?" Esther liked the young production assistant. Knowing her salary was small, she always gave Ellen a discount.

"I want the works, Esther," came the answer. "Money is no object."

"Oh?" Esther said, her eyes sparkling. "Big date tonight?"

"I guess you could say that," Ellen said softly, looking down as she blinked back tears. She passed the open book to Esther. "Can you make me look like this?"

Esther gazed down at the page and stifled a giggle. "What's this?" She looked at the book cover. "Sleeping Beauty? I haven't thought about Sleeping Beauty since I was twelve. She is pretty, though. That's how you want me to do your hair?"

Ellen blushed. "It's a special occasion," she said softly.

Esther smiled, "You're going to look gorgeous, my dear."

An hour later, as Ellen was leaving The Beautiful You, she hugged the hairdresser tightly. "Thank you, Esther, I hope you'll never forget me," she said, tears coursing down her cheeks.

"Forget you, dear? Never. I love you like a daughter. Why are you crying? Are you leaving us?"

Looking intently in Esther's eyes, Ellen said, "I can promise you Esther, I'll always be here."

"That's wonderful, dear. I would miss you," Esther said, giving Ellen's hair a final pat. "Have a good time on your date."

Back at her cottage, Ellen filled three large bowls to the brim with Cat Chow as the little calico rubbed against her legs. Her mind drifted back to that day last February. Coming home, she had hurried to get in out of the frigid weather. She paused at the door, thinking she heard something. A tiny but persistent meowing came from under the bush beside the house. Bending down, she reached in and wrapped her hand around the shivering bundle of curled up fur. She carried the frozen kitten into the kitchen. Holding him to her breast, she heated a pan of milk.

Tonight as she cuddled the cat she whispered to him, "You're so beautiful. Esther is going to love you." Setting him down, Ellen sat at the table and wrote a short note to Esther. She put it under the sugar bowl where she knew they would find it.

After changing the litter box, she stood before the mirror and carefully eased the satin and lace wedding gown over her head. She had bought the dress three years before, feeling sure she would find a husband among the members of Grace Tabernacle. Grabbing a tissue, she dabbed at the tears spilling down her cheeks.

In the bathroom, she opened the medicine chest and reached for the bottle of sleeping pills. As her fingers touched it, a crushing sadness made her breath catch. All her dreams were gone, vaporized in a cloud of nothingness. Her loving husband, their beautiful children, their happy home. Gone, gone forever.

She looked down and placed her hand gently on her stomach. "Don't worry, little one, soon Jesus will hold you in His arms and be a much better father to you than... than... Robert." Sobs shook her body.

She opened the bottle and pressed the rim against her lips. With her eyes squeezed tightly shut, she paused for a few seconds, then upended the container and swallowed the 30 remaining pills. She gasped and gripped the edge of the sink, then gulped down a big glass of water. The last of the pills sticking in her throat finally slid down. After dabbing at the redness in her eyes, she reapplied her makeup.

By the time she finished, she was rocking with wooziness. Using the wall for support, she stumbled to the bedroom. Collapsing on the bed, she collected herself enough to fan out the billowing skirt and spread her hair across the pillow. Still licking his chops, the cat hopped on the bed and curled up at her hip. For a few minutes, she stroked his back and smiled faintly as he rewarded her with his loud purring. When he was asleep, she clasped her hands over her stomach and waited.

The glow started in the corner of the room and radiated out until she was enveloped in a magnificent shimmering brilliance. The Man stepped through the wall, his garment shining with a heavenly light. A golden belt encircled his waist. Gripped tightly in his hand was the jewel-encrusted shaft of a gleaming sword. Ellen smiled. "My knight in shining armor. I had no idea you would be an angel." She closed her eyes and never opened them again on this earth.

# Chapter 6

Anne returned to her suite at the Ritz Carlton. Her spirits were soaring. She felt as if a giant eagle had swooped down, caught her up and carried her off to freedom. After years of captivity, the whole sky was her home.

For years, David had insisted she book no more than one or two conferences a year. "We need you here, dear," he said when she showed him her date book filling up with nearly back-to-back speaking invitations. "Overseeing the women's ministries is a big job and time consuming. You're a very valuable member of the staff."

Of course, there were many times she went along with David to his conferences and, once they got there, was asked to speak also. But she was always, always in his shadow. No more. She would not be an afterthought. She would not be held down. Robert's wife, May, had taken the position of women's ministry coordinator three months ago, leaving Anne free to travel.

From the moment she deplaned, the leadership of Women's Rejoice treated her like royalty. She was breath taken by the stretch limo at the airport, the two dozen red roses and huge basket of fruit in the luxurious Ritz Carlton suite and the hotel staff members falling all over themselves to accommodate her.

As she stepped off the escalator at the airport, Anne giggled with nervous excitement. There holding a sign with her name was a chauffeur who in his former life must have been a linebacker in the NFL. The bulge at his side was not a cell phone. Bowing at the waist, he said, "My name is Reggie, Mrs. Padgett. I'll be assisting you during your stay in Atlanta. If'n you need anything, anything at all, you just let me know." His attempt to smile reminded Anne of an origami project gone wrong.

"Thank you, Reggie," she said, holding out her hand. She expected him to kiss it. Instead, he gave it a firm shake.

She settled back in the seat of the limo as Reggie maneuvered expertly through the heavy traffic.

At the convention center, Reggie employed a threatening scowl to clear a path through the milling attendees as he briskly led Anne straight to the platform. As they passed, several women looked their way in startled delight and started toward her, some with wide open arms. One look from Reggie sent them scurrying back to their places.

The $12,000 honorarium couldn't compare to her husband's fee for a speaking engagement. However, the money was hers to do with as she pleased. She was just hours away from picking up the Roadster. Waiting on the platform for her introduction, she closed her eyes. The audience's buzz faded away as she slid behind the wheel. Yes! she exclaimed in her head, mentally driving her fist in the air.

When the chairwoman of Women's Rejoice introduced her, the standing-room-only crowd erupted in a roar. The applause seemed endless. Then, some of the women in the far left corner began stomping their feet. The jarring vibrations felt like an earthquake to Anne.

Slowly, the music swelled and the overwrought audience respectfully quieted down. As she approached the podium, Anne's eyes swept the arena as tears trickled from their corners. Three thousand women stood, eyes closed, hands raised in praise. "He is Lord!" Anne called into the microphone, nearly swooning with emotion. The sea of beaming faces blurred before her. These women were so inspired, so on fire. They adored…Her! She was a queen and never again would she allow David to keep her out of the public eye.

Relaxing later in her quiet suite, Anne ordered room service and asked that the meal be delivered in an hour. After a long bath, she sat down to a sirloin steak festooned with a dizzying array of elaborately prepared vegetables. It was too much food. After finishing what she could, she sat on the sofa and opened her briefcase.

When they left the arena, Anne asked Reggie to take her on a little tour of the city. He gladly complied, driving slowly and pointing out various landmarks. While he was distracted, she slipped a bottle of champagne out of the limo's refrigerator and placed it on the floor. Squeezing it between her feet, she opened her briefcase and pushed it off her lap. Maneuvering the bottle with her feet, she slid it into the opening, then subtly reached down and quietly closed the zipper.

Now she poured a small amount into a plastic glass and set it on the coffee table. For a few long moments, she stared at the tiny, inviting bubbles. Finally, she raised the glass. The bubbles tickled her upper lip. It tasted good. She was surprised at its smoothness. She felt soooo wicked.

All her life she had heard of the evils of liquor from her father, her pastor and her husband. Nothing prepared her for this buzz. After two more glasses, she was lightheaded. Thoughts sped through her head like a runaway train. One speaking engagement a month wasn't enough. She would schedule more. If David didn't like it, tough. He could have his life and she'd have hers.

A book! That's what she needed. A book would open all kinds of doors. Anne Beth Padgett, author. She liked the sound of it. What about a title? She needed a gripping title. "Living in the Shadow of the Almighty," she said aloud, surprised to hear herself slurring. Self-consciously, she murmured, "Maybe I should tone it down a bit. `The Wife of David Padgett.' No, I don't think so!" She giggled and tumbled into an easy chair, splashing champagne on the carpet. Living in the shadow of greatness. "That's it! 'Living in the Shadow of Greatness'! Subtitle: 'My Life as the Wife of David Padgett'. No. 'David Padgett's Wife has a Life'." She snickered giddily. Fix it later.

For the next hour, she interspersed writing and polishing off the bottle. Then she licked the cork and banged her head on the desk as she went to lay it down. "Congratulations to me," she snuffled. With her arms dangling at her sides, she passed out.

Somewhere deep in her dream the phone rang.

Didn't the maid realize she was exhausted from her book tour and speaking engagements? Why didn't she answer that infernal ringing? It finally stopped. "Thank you, Sarah," she mumbled.

Sometime later, there was knocking at the door. "Just tell them I'm too busy to speak to them, Jane," Anne muttered without raising her head. The knocking became rapping, then pounding. Slowly, Anne roused and got to her feet. She groaned as the hammering sent a shooting pain through her brain. Her eyes fell on the empty champagne bottle on the floor. She had to get rid of it. Whimpering as she bent to pick it up, she stumbled to the bedside table, opened the drawer and tried to shove it to the back. It stuck. Something was in the way. Reaching in, she pulled out a Gideon Bible. Dropping it on the bed, she pushed in the bottle and slammed the drawer shut. She glanced at her wristwatch. Eight-forty AM. She was to be at a breakfast with the leadership at 8:30. Frantic, she forced her wobbly legs to carry her to the door and flung it open.

Reggie stood with his feet apart and his fist raised, ready to pound again. "Mrs. Padgett, are you all right?" he asked, masking his annoyance behind a look of concern. "The night clerk said he was told to wake you at six thirty, but he got no answer. He let it ring a long time."

"Yes, yes, of course, I'm fine. I'm so sorry for the trouble. I was up most of the night outlining a new book. I overslept." She turned her face away, hoping he wouldn't smell her breath.

"If you're ready, I'll escort you to the dining room."

"Just give me a minute to freshen up. Do you mind waiting out here?" Reggie folded his arms over his chest and leaned against the wall. She closed the door and hurried to the bathroom. Stepping to the sink, she tried unsuccessfully to wash the redness from her eyes. Rummaging through her purse, she pulled out her toothbrush and lipstick. She brushed for a full minute, then rinsed three times with Listerine. She held her hand in front of her mouth and winced. She'd let them do all the talking.

She looked in the full-length mirror at her clothes. A few wrinkles here and there. She wriggled out of her skirt and grabbed a fresh one from the closet, holding it against her hip in one hand while she ran a brush through her hair with the other. She dropped the brush and tried to steady her shaking fingers as she ran the lipstick around her mouth. Finally, she scrambled into the skirt and opened the door.

"All ready," she said, giving Reggie a weak smile. Still frowning, he pulled the door closed as she exited.

In the dining room, the Maître d' led her to a large round table surrounded by members of the conference leadership. An elderly, gray-haired woman in a frumpy floral print dress gave her a sour look. Anne recognized her as Rose Turner, the Women's Rejoice chairwoman who had introduced her at the conference.

"We weren't sure you would be joining us, Mrs. Padgett," she sniffed. She took a dainty sip of her orange juice. "We were just about to start without you."

"Did you oversleep after all the excitement yesterday?" the wife of a Christian radio talk show host queried, smiling sweetly and raising her eyebrows.

Anne hated her for that cloying smile. She wanted to slap the woman. She couldn't decide which one of these two phonies she disliked more. Her head throbbed, her eyes were blurry and bile rose into her throat. She swallowed, hoping to keep the nausea down. She took a sip of water and forced a smile. "Oh, no," she said, drawing out the words. "I was up most of the night outlining a new book."

"How exciting," the chairwoman said sarcastically as she rolled her eyes. "May I ask what it's about?"

Anne wracked her brain but for the life of her could not recall a single point of the outline. "I'd rather not say just yet," she fudged, trying to maintain her smile. The muscles in her face ached; indeed, her whole body hurt. "I'm sure you

42

understand. Just as an artist will not allow someone to view his painting until it is complete."

The women all nodded in agreement. All, that is, except Rose Turner. "It seems to me if a person is writing a book they should be proud of it," she snipped. "That is, unless you're writing something you're ashamed of." Anne wanted to wring the old hag's neck. Even if she'd had the nerve, she didn't have the strength.

The rest of the day was a miserable ordeal. Several times, she had to run to the ladies' room. Each visit brought up more of her small breakfast. The banquet at noon was excruciating. The smell of food made her retch and the noisy chatter made her head pound mercilessly. Throughout the day, she repeatedly swore both at and off alcohol. When she stood to close the conference, her knees felt as if they would buckle. At her introduction, the women once again began stomping their feet. They may as well have been stomping on her head. Gripping the edges of the podium, she was able to slowly regain her equilibrium. Her hands still shook, but her voice became stronger as she ad-libbed her closing speech. She remembered how David ended his sermons. Wrapping up the lecture, she looked down, then began to sing in a low, throaty voice, "He is Lord, He is Lord, He has risen from the dead, and He is Lord."

Taking their cue, the musicians began to play. Without waiting to be invited, women streamed down the aisles in droves. Turning her face from Rose Turner's view, Anne held up her Bible as she led the singing. A glossy brochure slipped from its pages. She glanced down at the picture of a baby blue Mercedes Roadster.

# Chapter 7

Growing up in relative isolation on a farm, David was withdrawn. His mother tried to help him overcome his shyness by inviting children from their church to come over and play. David would engage with them for a brief time, then disappear into the woods until his playmates became discouraged and went home. Any time a vehicle came down the gravel road, he would duck behind the house or anything handy that would hide him. It took him years to overcome this difficulty. Even today, remnants of the problem remained.

When David graduated from college, he couldn't wait to pastor his own church. He came alive each time he stood in the pulpit. It was as if an electrical current coursed through him. Behind the pulpit, he took on a strikingly different persona. He spoke with an authority that commanded the attention of his listeners. Now he was bored with preaching. It was just another task to be mechanically performed. Whether he lost his fire suddenly or over time he could not say.

Book signings were the worst. With nothing but a table and a pen between him and his clamoring admirers, he labored to steady his trembling hands and racing heart. Dealing one-on-one with people unnerved him. Writing, however, was something he always enjoyed.

Most pastors dreaded Monday mornings. They were a soul-flattening letdown after the exuberance of a full day of worship. David, however, looked forward to them. After the weekly staff meeting, he would retire to his office and write for several hours. His secretary had standing orders not to disturb him unless it was a dire emergency. Clicking away at his computer, David could create a world where peace and harmony reigned, an atmosphere totally antithetical to the world in its depraved condition. This morning, though, he couldn't concentrate. He phrased the same sentence four different ways and still it felt stiff and lifeless.

Leaning back in his chair, David thought of his first book. Flush with the success of his burgeoning church, he had written it over an eight-month period. But throughout that time its title escaped him. He searched his mind over and over. He needed something so compelling it would fairly jump from the shelf into a Christian's hands. The very first page would change the way the reader viewed his or her own church. Finally, he had it. He called it "Seed Church", the message being that Christians must die to self in order to reach the world. Toward the end he worked on the manuscript until one or two in the morning. When he was satisfied, he gave it to Anne to read.

So as not to disturb her perusal, he waited in the church for three hours, anxiously pacing the floor. He would plunk down in a pew only to jump up within a few seconds and pace some more. When he couldn't stand it any longer, he ran back to the house. Anne sat on the sofa dabbing her eyes. "I'm so proud of you," she said, hugging him tightly. "It's a wonderful book. It will change the world."

Emboldened by her praise, he sent 29 query letters to agents listed in the Writer's Market. Shuffling through the mail three weeks later, his heart skipped a beat. "Anne, Anne, come in here!" he shouted.

"What is it, what's wrong?" she cried as she rushed from the kitchen.

With trembling fingers he held up the envelope from a New York agent. A grin spread broadly over Anne's face. "Well, author David Padgett, open it. Let's see how much I can spend at Saks."

"I can't. Here," David said, handing her the envelope. Needing no coaxing, Anne tore it open and pulled out a single sheet of paper. As her eyes flew down the page, her face fell and tears began to glisten.

His smile gone, David took the letter from her. He looked incredulously at his own query letter. Scrawled across the bottom were the words, "Not for us."

Over the next two months, 27 more form letters came in the mail. 'Too preachy'. 'Too long'. 'Too short'. He threw them away without bothering to read any further. Each envelope that landed in the mailbox brought a thrill. Each rejection tore out his heart. After the 27th, he locked himself in his office and cried like a baby.

When the 28th arrived, he thought it was an advertisement for Sunday school literature. Anne picked it out of the wastebasket. "What's this?" she asked, turning it over in her hand.

"Oh, just some junk mail."

"David, this is addressed to you. It's from the editor of Blessings Publishing House." She handed it to him. The words burned through his soul.

*Dear Rev. Padgett,*

*Your book 'Seed Church' appears to have tremendous potential.*

*Please send us the completed manuscript as soon as possible. We will review it carefully.*

*Wishing you the best,*

*Ed Holt, Senior Editor*
*Blessings Publishing House*

Re-reading the manuscript before sending it, David knew he could improve it. Using the original as a guide, he worked around the clock. Over the next few days, he barely ate or slept. When the words would blur on the page, he took short catnaps.

Saturday morning, David rushed into the post office. In his haste, he stumbled on the door jamb. Sorting mail behind the counter, Bill Decker looked up, startled. "Why Pastor, you feeling okay? You're white as a sheet," he said, reaching for the package in David's outstretched hand. "You look like you're about ready to collapse."

"Just tired, Bill," David said, handing the manuscript to the postmaster. Releasing his grasp on it, he felt as if he was sending his only child off to war.

For the next two weeks he heard nothing. Anne wanted to share the news with her friends but he swore her to secrecy. Every morning he walked to the post office and hung around while Bill sorted the mail and filled the boxes. Finally, three weeks later, the package came. David's heart raced as Bill handed him the brown parcel. "Is this what you've been waiting for, Pastor?"

"Yes, thanks," he murmured. The lump in his throat was as big as a baseball. Hidden from the world in his church office, his shaking hands tore open the wrapping. The cover letter with no check attached sent a knife through his heart.

*Dear Rev. Padgett,*

*Thank you for giving us the opportunity to review your manuscript. I'm afraid we will have to pass on it. Unfortunately, the book didn't live up to our expectations. Perhaps you might consider taking a writing course at your local college. I wish you the best in your further endeavors as an author.*

*Sincerely,*

*Ed Holt, Senior Editor*
*Blessings Publishing House*

Walking crestfallen back to the house, David went straight to the living room and collapsed in the Lazy Boy. He buried his face in his hands as Anne stepped into the room, wiping her hands on a dish towel. She glanced down at the letter on the coffee table. "I'll never make it," David moaned. "I might as well give up."

47

Playing on the floor with his toy truck, Bobby's eyes widened as he watched and listened to his daddy.

"Honey, listen to me," Anne said, her eyes moistening. "You'll find a publisher and your book will be a best seller. I know it."

David jumped up, nearly tripping over the little boy. "No!" he exploded. "Stop talking like that. I don't need or want false hope. It's no good, I'm no good, my writing's no good!" Grabbing the manuscript, he marched into the kitchen and threw it in the trash. It sank down among the coffee grounds and pasta sauce.

Anne, dear sweet Anne. Her faith in him kept him going through those hard first years. After he left the house to take a walk, she fished the manuscript out of the garbage. She hid it in the bedroom closet, taking it out only when he wasn't home. David didn't speak of it again. That chapter of his life was closed.

Over the next few days, Anne re-typed the soiled pages. Twenty miles from Grafton, she waited at a Staples store while the kid behind the counter printed five copies of the manuscript. Then she sent them via Federal Express to publishers she found in a book at the library.

The call came six weeks to the day after David threw the manuscript away. He savored that conversation word-for-word as if it were yesterday. He remembered lifting the receiver reluctantly, thinking it was probably another call for a hospital visit.

"Hello?"

"Reverend Padgett?" The voice had a kind of tinny, far-off quality.

"Yes?"

"This is Adam Watson with West Coast Publishing. I read your book 'Seed Church' and I must say I loved it. It's insightful, spirited. It's a great tool for Christians seeking to impact their city for the Lord." David stood gripping the phone, his mouth agape.

"What is it?" Anne asked.

48

Covering the mouthpiece, David mouthed "Book." Anne's face split in a wide grin. Watson was still talking.

"I know ten thousand isn't much of an advance. However, it's just an advance. I can assure you unequivocally, your book will fly to the top of the bestseller list. I'm sending you a contract. I want you to read it thoroughly and carefully before you sign. Is this satisfactory with you?"

Sputtering, David found his voice. "Yes, yes, of course. I'm glad you liked my book," he said with a lump in his throat.

"Oh, it's a wonderful book, truly. It will take the Christian world by storm. Sign the contract and send it back right away. We need to get cracking on it. Again, Reverend, wonderful book. Goodbye."

Still gripping the receiver, David turned in shock to his wife. Standing at the sink, dishcloth in hand, she smiled at him. Then he understood. "You, it was you," he said, his voice cracking, tears running down his cheeks. "But how? I don't understand. I threw it in the garbage. There was gunk all over it."

"And I rescued it, sweetheart," she said, taking him in her arms. "I retyped it and sent it off."

"No dear, you didn't rescue the book," he said, hugging her tightly. "You rescued me."

Just as Watson predicted, within six weeks of its release, *Seed Church* reached the top of the Christian bestseller list. That was 19 years and seven bestsellers ago. Now it was only through his books that David came alive as he had in the pulpit in times past.

Crossing to the glass wall, David gazed out at the grounds. Swans glided on the mirror surface of the lake. The branches of the dogwoods and Japanese maples swayed in the gentle breeze. On the walking path, a jogger passed a young couple holding hands. The fountain's spray bent the sunlight into delicate rainbow pastels.

Despite the wonderment spread out before him, a frown marred David's visage. His life was the envy of every pastor in America. He had a beautiful wife, a son being groomed to follow in his footsteps, TV and radio ministries reaching millions around the world. Pre-orders for his new book exceeded all the others. Why was he so unhappy?

Back at his desk, David continued writing. Forty-five minutes later, his secretary buzzed him. "Sorry to disturb you, Pastor," she said. "Mrs. Padgett is here."

"Send her in, Shirley," David said, wondering why Anne would disturb his writing. When the door opened, he was surprised to see May. His daughter-in-law rarely came to his office, and never when he was writing.

Stepping from behind the desk to greet her, he could see she was fighting back tears. "May, what is it, what's wrong?" he asked. Taking her hand, he led her to the couch. As they sat down, May began to sob. Pulling an envelope out of her jacket pocket, she thrust it at him.

Silently, David pulled the sheet of paper from the torn edge of the envelope. Something weighty was between the folds. Opening it up, he saw a key taped below the writing. His stomach began to churn as he read the shaky lines.

*Dear Rev. Padgett,*

*You may not remember me. My name is Ellen Ridgeway. I am one of Grace Tabernacle's production assistants. We met briefly at last year's Christmas party. What I have to tell you is very painful. Please don't misunderstand me, I'm not writing you out of revenge. I feel very strongly that God is using you and Grace Tabernacle for good. Therefore, I'm trying to avoid a scandal.*

*I am sending a copy of this letter to Robert so the two of you can work this out. Well, there is no other way to say it. I'm pregnant with Robert's child. Unfortunately, he refuses to discuss the matter with me. Therefore, after much thought I have decided the only way out is to take my life and the life of the baby. I believe if I aborted this dear child, I would be a murderer worthy of death.*

50

*Please don't be angry with me, I feel this is the only way. One final request, don't let Robert attend my funeral.*

*Good bye,*
*Ellen Ridgeway*

The room was spinning. David gripped the letter to keep from dropping it.

May's eyes were dry now. "Oh, Dad," she said, her voice cracking, "what are we going to do?" She stood up and began pacing. "Oh, this poor, deluded girl. For her to accuse Robert of being the father of her baby." She stopped and looked at David. "Do you believe her?"

"Of course not. Calm down, May, we'll handle—"

The door burst open. Robert rushed in holding a letter. He stopped in his tracks at the sight of his wife. The young pastor stared at her. Something passed between them.

"It's true, isn't it?" May demanded.

"No, no, of course not," Robert lied, wiping his upper lip with the back of his hand. "It's just the delusions of a psychopath."

"Robert, don't," May said sharply. She grasped the edge of the desk to steady herself. Her voice became strident. "Don't lie to me. I'm your wife, don't you dare lie to me!"

Robert ignored her. "Dad, if she's committed suicide, we need to distance ourselves from this."

"Yes, yes, of course," David said, too stunned to think. He stared at Robert, trying to read his eyes. He tried to convince himself he had to protect the church and the ministry. A chill ran through him—this could hurt the sale of his new book.

"You can't be serious. You're putting public relations over the welfare of this woman and her baby? "May looked in amazement from Robert to her father-in-law.

51

"May, be reasonable." Robert reached out and put his hand over hers. "If this girl has taken her life, there's nothing we can do," he said.

"I want an answer!" she shouted, wrenching away her hand. "Did you make love to this woman?"

Robert's face reddened. He was angry, not ashamed. "All right, if you must know, she forced herself on me," he said. He stood there stone-faced as David and May struggled to digest his admission.

May sat down next to David. "I know who this girl is, Robert. A little thing like her 'forcing' a big strong guy like you to have sex with her? You're a liar."

David tried to speak, but words wouldn't come.

"And you expect me to believe all those shopping trips were with your girl friends?" Robert countered, rudely mimicking her inflection as he cocked his head from side to side.

"Call them. Angie and Rose. Go ahead. Their numbers are right here," May said, taking her cell phone from her pocket and thrusting it at her husband's face.

"Right, you're as pure as the driven snow."

May jumped up and stormed toward him, scooping the phone off the floor. "Do you want to call them or should I? And I'll tell them why you're asking," May said, punching in numbers.

Yanking the phone from her hand, Robert threw it against the bookcase. It bounced off David's copy of *Gone With the Wind* and fell at May's feet. Bending at the knees, she picked it up and stuck it in her pocket. David sat silent, blanching at the tension.

Her face expressionless, her lips a thin, tight line, May straightened up and faced her husband. "I want a divorce," she stated woodenly. "And believe me, it won't be a quiet one." She turned toward the door. Robert stepped into her path. David's blood ran cold. This could be the deathblow to his ministry.

"Get out of my way," May said in a low, menacing growl.

"Not until you calm down." There was dead silence as they stared each other down.

May thought she was seeing her husband for the worm he really was. She tilted back her head, gave him a big, broad smile and asked quite sweetly, "You know why I'm glad this happened now?" When there was no response, her voice turned as hard as a hammer on a nail and she told him, "Because not having children will make the divorce so much simpler."

This had gone far enough. Stepping between the warring couple, David said, "There's not going to be any divorce." May glared incredulously at her father-in-law. "Robert's right," he continued, his voice trembling. "May, think of all the people it would hurt. The new Christians, the teenage girls you work with, your own ministry to the women."

At heart May was a good woman, giving to the needy, helping at the homeless shelter, counseling the teenage girls. David knew he had hit where she hurt.

"I need some air." Pushing past Robert, May rushed from the room, ignoring the startled secretary's good-bye.

Robert heaved a sigh as he turned to his father. "We have to keep this quiet."

"I agree, "David said, fighting back his disgust. He really didn't need this right now, or ever. "As distasteful as this situation is, it's best for the church if it doesn't come to light." Checking his wristwatch, David quietly cracked open the door and peeked out. "Shirley's on her break. Let's go out the back way."

Now where do you s'pose them preachers are going in such an all-fired hurry? Rex Mullins wondered as he leaned on his rake. He watched the Mercedes speed out of the parking lot and down the street.

# Chapter 8

As David wheeled the Mercedes onto Third Street, the dreary sky let loose with a torrent of rain. Sweat beads glistened on his forehead. "Son, now that I'm thinking about it, this isn't right. We should let the police handle this."

Robert looked extremely agitated. "And what if she left another note, Dad?" he snapped. "What if she left one implicating me in her house?" He slouched down in the passenger seat, jiggling his knees. "All we have to do is search the house and leave. If we find any more notes, we'll destroy all of them."

David was fed up with the whole business. "If you had controlled yourself, this wouldn't have happened!" he yelled, his face flushed with anger. "This is not the way I taught you to conduct yourself."

"Taught me?" Robert yelled back. "I barely saw you from the time I was seven. All you ever taught me was that your ministry comes before family, friends, or even the Lord."

David's face stung as if it had been slapped. "Son, you know that's not true," he said, knowing in his heart it was. "We'll discuss it later."

How many times has he said that to me? Robert thought. Later never comes.

David slowed down and turned into the alley behind Ellen's house. Creeping along, they approached her driveway. The rusty Escort sat in the back yard where she parked it Friday evening. Locking the car, David and Robert hurried to the back door. David's hand shook so hard he couldn't insert the key. Finally, Robert snatched it from his father's hand and opened the door.

They saw it immediately, a letter-sized sheet of paper underneath the sugar bowl. The air in the house reeked of cheap perfume and death. David held his handkerchief over his nose. Shock and sadness overtook him. "What have you done, Robert? What have you done?" he implored in a scratchy whisper.

Robert grabbed the sheet of paper. "I'm gonna look in her bathroom. Check the rest of the house," he ordered in a savage tone David had never heard. He stepped into the living room and glanced around. His eyes froze on the open door to his left. He saw Ellen on the bed. Holding the handkerchief more tightly to his face, he crept closer.

She lay there still and gray in a beautiful white wedding gown. She looked like a child playing dress up. Her face was peaceful. A sad smile curled the edges of her mouth. A diamond ring two sizes too big hung on her left ring finger. Overcome with anguish and disbelief, David braced himself on the headboard. The handkerchief fell from his face as he picked up her hand. He gagged. A sob broke through. "Oh you poor, poor girl, please forgive us."

He tried to pray. Tears ran down his cheeks and fell onto her lace sleeve. He was vaguely aware of an urgent whispering behind him. "Dad, the police are here!" Then he heard the knock.

"Grafton Police! Miss Ridgeway? Can you come to the door?" The knocking came again. Panicked and disoriented, David let Ellen's hand drop. The ring fell from her finger onto the floor.

"Come on, Dad, we've got to get out of here!" Robert hissed. Snatching up the handkerchief, Robert jammed it into David's pocket. He grabbed David's arm, pulled him toward the doorway and literally dragged him through the house. Terrified by the sudden noises, the cat fled under the bed. They stumbled out the back door, closing but not locking it.

The splattering rain quickly brought David out of his haze. The two men raced to the car. Robert jumped into the passenger seat and quietly closed the door. A dog barked. Climbing in behind the wheel, David started the motor and eased the car into the alley. Just as the car's back end disappeared behind the garage, a police officer opened Ellen's kitchen door. Three blocks away, David pulled the car to the curb and stopped. "We have to go back."

"And do what, Dad? Introduce myself to the police?" "Hi, Officer. Who am I? Oh, just the father of her baby. I'm the reason she killed herself."

David was flabbergasted by his son's cold sarcasm. He sighed heavily. "Think logically son, there won't be any autopsy. I'll speak to the mayor. Without an autopsy, without the suicide notes, no one will know you were the father—" David's cell phone interrupted. He flipped it open.

"Pastor Padgett? Pastor, there's been a horrible tragedy," Shirley sobbed. This couldn't be happening. How could she have learned of this so quickly?

"What happened?" David was a novice at feigning ignorance. Shirley's sobbing made her words incoherent. "Take a deep breath and speak slowly," David said, trying not to sound impatient.

"Mrs. Padgett," she wailed.

"Anne? What about Anne?" David shouted as Robert looked at him wide-eyed.

"No, no," Shirley sniffled. "Mrs. May. She... her... car went off the highway and hit a tree. Oh, Pastor. Oh, dear Lord. She was killed instantly."

David screamed and dropped the phone. He buried his face in his hands and leaned on the steering wheel, heaving with sobs.

Robert was in a frenzy. He pushed at his father's arm and yelled, "Dad? Dad! What is it? What's wrong? Is Mother all right?"

Raising his head, David looked at his son. "It's May."

"Wha... what about May? Did she show someone the letter?"

"She was in an accident," David said as Robert swam before his eyes. "I'm sorry, son. She hit a tree."

"A tree... How...Where... Dad, speak to me!"

David laid his hand on Robert's arm."I'm so sorry, son. She's dead."

"What? Oh, my God. No, no, she can't be!" Robert screamed and dissolved in tears. David watched helplessly as his son shook with sobs. Then for a moment there was stillness. Robert rubbed his shirt sleeve across his face. Coldness spread across his red face. "God killed her. He hates me, he hates me."

Stunned, David struggled to say some words of comfort. He tried to calm his roiling mind and think of some scripture, a quotation to make it all go away. Words, even from scripture, seemed inadequate.

Slamming his fist into the dash, Robert screamed, "I hate you, God! Do you hear me? I hate you! I've got to get out of here." Wrenching open the door, he ran down the sidewalk. David sat quietly for several minutes, trying to gather his thoughts, trying to pray. His mind and heart were blank.

When Robert didn't return, David started the engine. A sharp rap on the window startled him. A state trooper gazed through the window, rain spilling off the brim of his smoky bear hat. David's heart pounded as he lowered the glass.

"Reverend Robert Padgett?"

"No Officer, I'm David Padgett. Robert is my son," David's hands were clammy. He could almost feel the handcuffs being clamped onto his wrists.

The trooper's eyes were sympathetic, his voice dispassionate. "Your daughter-in-law. I'm sorry, sir, she's—

"My secretary called a few minutes ago,"

"I'm sorry for your loss. Is there anything I can do?"

"No, sir, thank you anyway. I need to tell my wife before she finds out from the media."

Nodding, the trooper returned to his patrol car. After a few minutes, David started the car and drove around looking for Robert. After circling several blocks, he was becoming frantic. How could you tell if someone was suicidal? As he turned another corner, he spotted Robert coming out of a drug store.

"I was worried about you, son," David said as Robert slid into the passenger's seat.

57

"I called my mother," Robert said flatly.

"It's a shock to all of us," David said, fumbling for some meaningful words.

"She's not at the church."

"Where is she?"

"Her cell phone's shut off. I called the house. According to Sarah, she's picking up her new car," Robert said bitterly. For the first time in their 26 years of marriage, David hated his wife.

# Chapter 9

Jenny handled each call with the same script: "Reverend Padgett is very distraught over the deaths of his daughter-in-law and Ellen Ridgeway. He asks that you please respect the family's privacy as they grieve for their loved ones. He will hold a press conference at a later date."

David avoided the media until after May's funeral and he had met with the church's attorney. As a member of Grace Tabernacle, Paul Levy had a stake in the situation's outcome. However, fearing the appearance of conflict of interest and the potential loss of clientele, he had no choice but to refer David to another attorney.

David was aware he had to be honest with Paul. However, he could not force himself to bring up Ellen's pregnancy. His influence with the mayor had averted an autopsy. Ellen's body was shipped back to her small hometown in southern Illinois without any brouhaha.

Cringing at the thought of even a brief interaction, David bit the bullet and called Ellen's mother. "Ellen loved Grace Tabernacle almost as much as she loved the Lord," Mrs. Ridgeway said, her voice thick with tears. "And she loved you, Reverend." There was a pause. "Do you have any idea why she would take... her... life?" She broke into sobs.

David's hands went clammy, his pulse quickened. "No, Mrs. Ridgeway, I'm sorry," he said, hating the lie and himself.

"Forgive me. I know you have your own loss to deal with. Thank you for all you did for my darling little girl." She hung up before David could reply      "I believe May took her own life." When David dropped the bombshell the day after the funeral, Anne held up better than he expected.

"Oh, come on David, that's crazy. That pathetic little Ellen I can understand. But May? No, it was just her time. As tragic as it is, we have to accept it and help Robert get through it."

59

David sat silent, dreading telling her. Keeping his eyes down, he finally said, "She killed herself within hours of learning of Robert's... infidelity." Hearing nothing, he looked up, searching Anne's face and shocked at her lack of emotion.

She began to pace, tapping her chin with her finger. "If you're right, we have to put the right spin on this."

"The right spin?" David repeated angrily. What the...? You can't be serious, Anne. Our daughter-in-law is dead, an innocent woman killed herself and her unborn child and you're worried about spin?"

"Please, David, you must realize that it's best for the ministry. If it ever came to light... I must speak to Robert. If he slips—"

"Are you thinking of the ministry, or yourself?"

"I won't dignify that foolish statement with a reply. Did you destroy the suicide notes?" Anne asked, perching on the edge of David's desk.

"Honestly, I don't know. In the confusion I may have thrown them away."

Anne began rummaging through his wastebasket. "They're not here."

"Anne, stop that," David snapped. Taking her by the arm, he steered her to the door. Once there, he said more gently, "We will weather this storm, Anne, and you're right, we'll just go back to our regular routine."

When Robert returned to his office at Grace Tabernacle two weeks later, his first order of business was with accounting. "These figures can't be right," he said, his eyes scanning the ledgers. He flipped through them again.

"Yes sir, er, Reverend, I'm afraid they are." Harvey Lee was a mousy little man with a rapidly balding head and thick glasses. He always felt intimidated in the strapping young pastor's presence.

"But these numbers are down ten percent from last year's," Robert said shrilly, throwing the sheets down on Harvey's desk. Skittering across the smooth surface, they fluttered to the floor like a flock of wounded birds.

Tensing, Harvey ran his hand over his balding scalp. "Sa...summer is always a slow time, people going on vacation, forgetting about the Lord," he said, twisting a button on his shirt.

"And here expenses are up twelve percent?"

"Yes, er, Reverend, they are. Costs have increased."

"So what do we do?" Robert demanded, leaning across the desk and glaring at the frightened little man. "Kidnap a baby, hold him for ransom, rob a bank?" Harvey began to laugh nervously. The look on Robert's face stopped him.

Harvey spoke without thinking. "Kill someone?"

"What was that?" Robert blustered, his face inches from Harvey's. Robert stared him in the eyes. Harvey blinked.

"We... we trust the Lord as we always have," Harvey squeaked, wishing he were somewhere, anywhere, else.

"The Lord? The Lord?" Robert shouted, slamming his fist down on Harvey's desk and cracking the glass overlay in a spider-web pattern. "Where was the Lord when May killed... died?" Terrified, Harvey shoved back his chair. Catching on the carpet, it flipped and banged to the floor with him in it. He scrambled clumsily to his feet.

"You better find a way to cover expenses or you're out of a job," Robert snarled. Turning on his heel, he stalked out and slammed the door behind him.

For the next 15 minutes, Harvey paced and twisted his buttons until one of them snapped and flew across the room. Then he picked up the phone. "Ask Reverend Robert to come into my office, please." Five minutes later Robert marched in.

"What, Harvey?" Robert asked crossly, assuming his warrior stance in front of the door.

"Your father's birthday is coming up soon. How about we send out an extra appeal?"

"Yes, yes that might work," Robert said as the wheels started turning. "Make it sound like this might be his last."

"What? Oh, no, I never meant that," Harvey protested as he shrunk back in fear of Robert's reaction. "I mean, we need the money, but to say he's dying? He'll never stand for that."

"Then we won't tell him, or my mother. Besides, you never heard me say Dad had cancer, did you?"

"Cancer? No, no, Reverend. But to even hint at such a thing in a letter…," Harvey's shirt was sticking to his back. "That could be considered mail fraud. I can't do it."

"Harvey, you will do it and I'll tell you why," Robert said, dropping into a visitor's chair and propping his feet on the bean counter's desk. "If you don't, I'll sign your name to it and send it out myself. Then I'll fire you and spread the word that you're not to be trusted. Now get busy and bring me that letter by the end of the day!"

Two hours later, Harvey meekly laid a typed sheet of paper on Robert's desk. Robert snatched it up and speed read it. "Not good enough," he said. Taking a pen, he added two lines. "Now it's ready." Reading Robert's edit, Harvey opened his mouth to object. "Send it, Harvey, or you won't be working as a janitor, let alone an accountant."

Back in his office, Harvey closed the door and sunk numbly into his chair. In his six years at Grace Tabernacle, no one had ever instructed him to do anything illegal. He slumped down on his knees. "Father, what would you have me do?" A verse from Proverbs entered his mind: The just man walketh in his integrity; his children are blessed after him. "But Lord," Harvey pleaded, "if I resign, where will I go?" The door opened and he jumped to his feet.

"You wanted to see me?" Jill Masterson stood in the doorway with a perturbed expression.

"I'm sorry, no. I didn't request a meeting with you."

"Reverend Robert said there was an urgent matter we needed to handle right away."

"Well, I," Harvey stammered, fearing the young pastor's intentions. Jill plunked down in the visitor's chair and studied her nails. "Can we move this along, Harvey? Bill and I have reservations at Mickardo's," she said, glancing at her wristwatch. Harvey handed Jill the letter.

"Is the pastor dying?" she asked casually after reading it.

"No, the report from his last physical said he was in excellent health," Harvey said.

As a member of the PR department and a paralegal, Jill knew the ropes. "Then to send this out would be to commit mail fraud."

"Reverend Robert wants it sent. I suppose we could go to Reverend David."

"And tell him what? That his son is coercing us into committing a felony? Hold on, I'll be right back." She rushed out of the office, returning minutes later with a massive law book under her arm. She slammed it down on the desk with a loud boom. Noticing the cracked glass top, she put her hand over her mouth. "Oh Harvey, I'm so sorry, did I do that?" she gasped.

"No, no, it happened this afternoon. Don't worry about it," Harvey said.

Opening the book, Jill ran her finger down the page and tapped at the paragraph that would get them off the hook. "Okay, look, if he insists on sending this letter to the people of Grace Tabernacle, have him sign a disclaimer. Here's how it should read." She glanced at her watch. "I have to go."

Harvey picked up the phone. "Leslie, is Reverend Robert still in his office?"

"No, I'm sorry, Mr. Lee, he just left If you'd like I'll try to catch him."

"No, thank you," Harvey said too quickly. "I'll see him first thing tomorrow."

"He won't be in tomorrow, sir," Leslie said. "He's playing in the charity golf tournament at Bridgeport. Of course, you could call his cell phone."

"Thank you, Leslie," Harvey said. Opening his desk drawer, he stared at the contents. He removed a few items and laid them on the ruined glass. After a few minutes, he put them back. From the third shelf of Harvey's bookshelf, David Padgett's smiling photo looked down at him. "Reverend Padgett's health is excellent for a man dying of heart disease," he murmured. Turning to his keyboard, Harvey began drafting the letter that could land him in federal prison.

Fortunately for Harvey, subsequent events caused Reverend Robert to forget all about it. It lay in a drawer in Harvey's desk and was never mentioned again.

# Chapter 10

In the skies over Pittsburgh, David fastened his seat belt. His schedule this week included conventions in the Steel City, Cleveland and Chicago. The flight was as smooth as silk, not a hint of turbulence and, of course, first class was the only way to go. David smiled, remembering those trips in coach. Invariably he would be stuck next to a bawling baby, a jovial storyteller whose love handle spilled into his seat, or a first-time flier retching with airsickness. Finishing his soda, David handed the empty glass to the attendant as they approached Pittsburgh International. He leaned back and closed his eyes, hoping to rest for a few more minutes. Suddenly the plane took a nosedive, lurching David against his seat belt. Losing her balance, the female attendant stumbled into his lap.

"I'm terribly sorry, sir," she said, regaining her footing. She fell over him again as the aircraft twisted sideways. The passengers screamed in terror as the plane whipped through the sky like a snake.

Outside the window, another 747 streaked past with flames shooting from its engines. David's heart leaped into his throat. Then, even as he watched the horror unfolding, his fear was replaced with peace, a calmness he hadn't felt in years. David could clearly see the terrified faces of the passengers as the crippled plane wobbled precariously as if in slow motion. An older couple clung together, an attractive woman in a business suit held her mouth open in a silent scream. A boy of five or six stared at him. David could see tears in his eyes. He mouthed words David couldn't decipher. He wanted to reach out and comfort the child, to tell the little boy everything would be all right. That was a lie. Nothing would ever be all right for them again.

Then the 747 was gone. Tearing off his seat belt, David bounded across the aisle to the window. Fifteen hundred feet below, the jet plummeted nose first to the ground. A huge fireball rose, shooting past the window. David's plane

65

shuddered as flames spread across its left wing. To David it appeared as if half the wing was gone. All that was left was jagged, torn metal. They began dropping. The screaming wind matched the shrieks of the passengers.

"Assume crash position!" the attendant shouted into the microphone at the front of the cabin.

Dropping into his seat, David yanked the seat belt around him and snapped it closed. Dropping his head between his knees, he saw death rushing up to meet him. In the back of the plane, a man began to loudly pray. His shouts carried over the chaos. "Oh Lord, send your angels to bear up your servants." There were more words, but David wasn't listening.

His thoughts went to his family. Would Anne get married again? The ministry would not miss a beat. Robert would eagerly step into his shoes. Would he be missed? Remembered? What of his life? Scenes flashed before him: entering the ministry, working day and night, his aspiration to reach the lost for Christ. In the last few years, his lust for money and power overtaking his life.

His life's work felt like cotton candy to him—sweet to the taste, melting away to nothing. He had squandered his existence. And what of the people in the other plane? Were they saved? Had God put someone in their path to plead the cause for Christ?

Tears for the little boy spilled from David's eyes. He would never know the joy of being married, of having children of his own. David became aware of flashes of light illuminating the cabin as the jet slowed and leveled off. David blinked, then gaped out the window, not believing what he was seeing. The fire on the wing was out. Surrounding the jet was a host of glowing beings.

In the cockpit, Captain Bernie Leonard struggled with the controls. They were hit, hit bad. The other plane filled his vision. It was going down, no way to save it, all hope gone. It was American Airlines Flight 980. The pilot was a close friend of Bernie's. Deep sorrow gripped his heart. There was no time to grieve; his own plane nose-dived.

66

"Part of the wing is gone, Captain! No way we can land her," the co-pilot shouted, his face chalk white.

Bernie grabbed for the mike. "Pittsburgh, this is Flight 276. We're going down. Repeat, Flight 276 going down!"

Sweat flowed from his brow into his eyes. He wiped it away with his sleeve. The closest he had ever come to a situation like this was when he was shot down over Vietnam. He ejected, his canopy floating him safely down to friendly territory. This time he would die, but not without a fight. He fought to restrain the wheel as it shuddered and shook like a machine gun.

The ground lights came at him like a freight train. Beside him the co-pilot screamed. A newlywed of six weeks, the younger man buried his face in his hands and sobbed.

"Pull up, pull up!" Bernie yelled at himself like a drill sergeant. With tears streaming down his face, the co-pilot took the mike and gave their location. Would their bodies be recognizable? Bernie wondered. Probably not. His would be a closed casket funeral. In his 20-year career with the airline, Bernie had attended several.

An old hymn came to his mind. Every week Miss Ursula insisted they sing it with gusto to open their Sunday school class. His five-year-old lungs nearly burst with the effort. He began to sing it now.

*Lord lift me up and let me stand*

*my feet on Heaven's tableland.*

*A higher plane than I have found,*

*Lord plant my feet on higher ground.*

An unearthly glow filled the cockpit. As if a giant hand had caught it, the plane stopped falling. The co-pilot began to laugh with giddy, high-pitched bursts of relief. The plane leveled off; the runway lights loomed straight ahead. At the edge of the runway, emergency vehicles waited, their flashing lights strobing like steady heartbeats. The touchdown was feather light. They came to a stop exactly where they should.

Bernie cried.

"Great flying, Captain, they should give you a commendation!" the co-pilot exclaimed, jumping from his seat.

"Son," Bernie said, his hands shaking, "God saved this plane, not me."

"Whatever you say, Captain," the young man said, grabbing his bag. "It's still great to be on terra firma."

In the cabin, David stood up and gripped the back of the seat in front of him. He watched as people young and old moved slowly down the aisle with smiles of relief. How could they be happy? Didn't they know the other plane exploded? No one could survive a crash like that.

The attendants repeated emergency deplaning instructions with mechanical efficiency to each passenger filing past. They're on auto pilot, he thought, and snickered a little before he caught himself. He saw the sorrow on their faces and the tears in their eyes. Regardless of their own terror and loss, they were expected to behave professionally. They would mourn their comrades later.

When David's turn came, the attendant from first class helped him onto the yellow chute. "Keep your legs spread," she ordered. It occurred to him to ask her if she was saved. Too late, he was sliding down the shoot. At the bottom, his wing tips dug into the concrete, scarring them. Two fire trucks roared past, racing to the other jet. In spite of their efforts, the fire prevailed. The stench of burning jet fuel and flesh filled the air.

A man in a business suit herded David and his fellow passengers toward a white bus. "What about the passengers in the other plane?" David asked him.

"I'm sorry, sir, there were no survivors," he answered sadly.

They were driven to a private lounge away from the news media. After giving their statements, they were ushered past the cameras. David tried to blend in, but a reporter recognized him. "Reverend Padgett! Reverend Padgett!" the excited man shouted. "Just a few questions, sir?"

"I'm sorry, not now," David answered, hurrying to the curb. A man in a chauffeur's cap stepped forward and steered him to a stretch limo.

At the Ritz-Carlton, David approached check-in. "Oh, Reverend Padgett, we are so glad you escaped injury," the smiling clerk gushed.

"Thank you," David murmured.

"Blaine," the man called out. A bellhop hurried to the desk. "Please take Reverend Padgett's luggage to the penthouse."

"I believe you've made a mistake," David told him. "My reservation is for a suite on the fifth floor."

"We upgraded you," the clerk said, smiling.

"Thank you," David said again.

"It's our privilege sir. And don't worry about the news people. Our staff has strict instructions not to speak to them." David nodded.

In the penthouse, David looked out on a stunning view of the Monongahela River and Station Square on its south bank. Traffic and pedestrians crossed the bridges, barges plied the water, people rushed to their destinations and activities without any thought of tomorrow. Life went on. For the families of the passengers lost in the crash, time stopped when their loved ones crossed into eternity.

"God, why did you spare me?" David cried aloud. Inside him, a still small voice answered, "Go ye into all the world and preach the gospel."

"What do you think I've been doing?" he argued with his unseen Lord. The voice was silent. "Preaching to hypocrites," David said, answering his own question. Preaching. The word hurt and left a bitter taste on his tongue. "Oh, Lord," he cried, "how could I have been so wrong?"

The phone rang. David stared at it as though it were a viper. On the tenth ring, he picked it up and slowly held it to his ear. "Hello?"

"David, is that you? You sound so odd," Anne said. His tongue tightened like a wet leather shoe. He didn't answer. What could he say to this woman, this stranger?

"David?"

"How am I supposed to sound, Anne? I almost died. I saw a planeload of people violently killed."

"I know, dear, we were praying for you," she said somberly. "Listen, David, we have a great opportunity here. I booked the Civic Arena for you tonight."

"Tonight, Anne? It's already two o'clock. I couldn't possibly preach. I—"

"I've been thinking," Anne went on as if she hadn't heard. "You should write a book about your experience. We could call it 'On Angel's Wings.' What do you think? The press is already buzzing about the title. Thanks to yours truly."

"Anne, Anne, a little boy died on that plane. A terrified elderly couple looked right into my eyes," David said, tears dripping off his chin. "Their plane came within fifty feet of mine. I couldn't save them. They died right in front of me."

"Wonderful, wonderful. Think of the drama that will add to the book. Write it down while it's still fresh in your mind," Anne said excitedly.

"I don't understand you, Anne. These were human beings. Their souls are somewhere at this very moment. Some of them are in hell."

Her tone went cold. "David, don't get crazy on me. People die every day. Where they choose to spend eternity is up to them."

"I can't preach tonight."

"Yes you can. David, this is huge. Ticket Master's already off the charts for tonight. Thousands of people want to hear about the miracle on Flight 276. That's how it's being billed. And who better than you to tell it? Don't disappoint me, David!" The dial tone buzzed in his ear.

# Chapter 11

Removing his jacket and tie, David eased down on the bed. Closing his eyes, he saw the older couple and the little boy in the doomed plane. The child's lips were moving. Tears came to David's eyes as a sweet, small voice came to him singing,

*Jesus loves me this I know*

*For the Bible tells me so*

*Little ones to him belong*

*They are weak but he is strong*

*Yes, Jesus loves me,*

*Yes, Jesus loves me,*

*Yes, Jesus loves me,*

*The Bible tells me so.*

He fell into the deep sleep of emotional exhaustion. In his dream, he saw the other plane descending. He felt the shudder as the two planes' wings touched. Once more, the angels came to his aid, bearing up the plane. He cried out. "Help them! Oh God, please don't let them die." Despite his pleas, the 747 plowed into the earth. A giant fireball rose from the wreckage.

This time, the flames engulfed David's plane. The clothing of the man across the aisle caught fire. "Help me, help me, I'm tormented by these flames!" he screamed. Flames shot from his eyes. The others crowded around David, their bodies ablaze, their flaming hands clawing at him.

The flight attendant grabbed him by the tie and pulled him close to her face. Her fiery eyes searched and seared his like branding irons. Her voice was shrill as a banshee's. "Why didn't you warn us? You knew we were on our way to hell!" Her flaming hands cupped his face. He felt no pain.

Fire leaping from their bodies filled the cabin. The smell of burning flesh made him gag. He gasped for air, choking on the acrid black smoke. Flaming hands grabbed at his arms and legs, tearing and burning through his clothes. He wrenched free. At the front of the plane he turned and faced them. Like ghouls in a horror movie, they rushed at him. The flames from their bodies ignited the seats and the top of the cabin.

Behind David the cockpit door opened. The pilot and co-pilot emerged, their blazing faces accusing him. "You didn't tell us, you didn't care," they chanted. They shrieked like the hounds of hell. "It's too late, it's too late." They cornered David, forcing his back against the exit door. The door flew open. Their faces filled with hate, the burning people pushed David into the open sky. He hurtled end over end through the air.

"No! No! No!" He woke up, sat bolt upright and looked all around, wrenching his head wildly from side to side. He was soaked with sweat. The room's ostentatious décor closed in on him. Anne's words nagged him. Don't get crazy on me, David! He must heed those words. After all, he had spent the last 20 years preaching happiness, prosperity and success. He had pulled her into that world with him. She, along with everyone else, expected him to be a rock in times of turmoil, always upbeat, always thinking good thoughts. Remember, God loves you. He wants you to enjoy the best life has to offer. Name it and claim it. When problems overtake you, face them with confidence knowing God will bring you through to a brighter day. Words, just so many empty words, He found no comfort in them, only more grief.

"Get ahold of yourself!" he yelled. He fell on his side and pulled the pillow under his quivering chin. "It wasn't real. It was just a nightmare."

72

Stripping off his sweaty clothing, David stepped into the shower. As the water cascaded over him, he recited his self-affirming incantation: "I am the best minister in the world. No one is better than I at preaching the gospel. People follow me wherever I go. They hang on my every word. I am the best at what I do. Yet every day, in every way, I am getting better and better."

He repeated it three times. Yet for all the words, he couldn't stop the tears. Out of the shower, he slowly regained his composure as he shaved, brushed his teeth and combed his hair. He opened his suitcase and selected a light blue suit, red tie and white Pierre Cardin shirt. White signifies integrity, or so the books say. Still wearing the hotel's robe, he called room service and ordered a small salad and a bottle of spring water, his normal fare before a speaking engagement. He wouldn't be speaking, but with the events of the day he knew he couldn't hold down a heavy meal.

He switched on the TV and flipped through the channels, stopping at CNN. He recognized the woman passenger who was sitting behind him. "Yes, Reverend Padgett was sitting right in front of me. I wanted to speak to him, but then again who am I? Just one of his minions."

"Do you believe God sent angels in answer to Reverend Padgett's prayer?"

"Absolutely. There was another man praying real loud in the back, but I'm sure God didn't hear him. It's like Reverend Padgett said in his book, *The Possibilities of God*: 'God's ear is closest to His leaders.'"

The smiling reporter turned to the camera. "And there you have it, a first-hand, eye-witness account of the miracle on Flight 276."

David hit the mute button and sat down at the desk. Using hotel stationary, he jotted down notes about the crash. Flipping through his Bible, he searched for relevant verses. His mind was blank. Oh, he quoted scripture in every service, but mostly to jump-start his preaching.

The knock on the door startled him. "Yes?"

"Room service, sir," a male voice answered.

"Of course," David said, opening the door.

A thirtyish man in a bellhop's uniform pushed a cart into the room. "Where would you like it, Reverend?"

"Just put it by the desk, yes, that will be fine." Facing David, the man hesitated. He smiled shyly and swallowed a couple of times. David grabbed his wallet off the dresser and pulled out a $10 bill. The bellhop held up his hand palm forward like a policeman halting traffic. He swallowed again. David saw that his eyes were glistening.

"I can't accept a tip from you, Reverend Padgett." David just stood there with the bill dangling from his hand. Had he offended this young man? "You see, twenty-five years ago you were part of an evangelism team at the Pacific Garden Mission in Chicago." Tears gathered in the man's eyes and spilled down his cheeks. "You led Bob Reed to Christ."

Bob Reed. David remembered, vaguely. The man was approximately the bellhop's age. His clothes were ragged and filthy, his breath stunk of vomit and liquor. David was as nervous as a new bride. In the class on evangelism, he had learned how to lead a soul to Christ. This was the first time he put it into practice. He was thrilled beyond belief when the man readily agreed to receive the Lord. David corresponded with Reed for a short time after, then lost track of him. It saddened him now to think of Bob Reed returning to his drunkenness. The lump in David's throat kept him from speaking.

"Dad became pastor of a small country church."

David looked wide-eyed at him and cleared his throat. "What church? Where? I would love to renew our acquaintance."

"Dad was in the World Trade Center on September eleventh. You see, a member of his congregation had a son who worked in the north tower. Dad and my mother went to New York with the father to visit him. The man was worried about his son's eternal destiny."

74

David's eyes were wet with tears. He knew the answer before he asked. "Did either of them survive?"

"Early that morning Dad met with the son at his office in the tower and led him to Christ. He called my mother back at the hotel to share the news. He was still on the phone with her when the plane hit."

"I'm sorry, so sorry," David said, mourning the loss of a friend he never knew.

"But it's all right, Pastor," Reed said, dabbing at his eyes with a white handkerchief. "Dad had a wonderful life. He died doing what he loved, witnessing for the Lord. He's in heaven today because of you."

David reached for the young man's hand and gripped it tightly. "Thank you, you have encouraged my heart."

Reed wiped his eyes. "I'm pastoring a small church outside the city. I would be honored if you would speak for us sometime," he said, handing David a gospel tract. "My home phone number and the service times are on the back."

"It would be my privilege, Bob," David said, looking down at the tract. He imagined trying to explain to Anne a speaking engagement that would garner no fee.

When Bob Reed Jr. was gone, David sat in deep thought in front of his untouched salad. How far he had come. He remembered how he and his fellow students bubbled over with excitement and anticipation as they prepared to minister in Chicago. On their first day of street preaching, the group of nervous young evangelists stayed close to the mission, never losing sight of one another. Emboldened by their common cause, they handed out tracts, witnessed and invited passersby to come to that evening's service. At the end of the day, they gathered at the mission for the harvest. Along with Bob Reed, that night five others trusted Christ. The elation on the way back to the college was at a fever pitch. David and his roommates stayed up half the night planning their futures.

David reached for his cell phone and punched in his secretary's home phone number. Blake Stains answered. "Hello, Blake, it's Pastor Padgett. Is Shirley there?"

"Yes, yes, Pastor. It's so good to hear your voice. Are you all right? It's all over the news about your plane being hit."

"Yes, Blake, thank you. I'm fine, just shaken up."

"Here's Shirley."

"Hello, Pastor! It's such a relief to hear your voice," Shirley said, her smile evident in her voice.

"Shirley, clear my schedule for the next few days. Have Robert take over the services."

"What should I tell the staff, the reporters? I've been checking voice mail at the church and they've been calling all afternoon."

"Just tell everyone I'm unavailable and you don't know my whereabouts."

"But Pastor..."

"Thank you, Shirley. I'll be in touch."

Fifteen minutes later his cell phone rang. "David, Shirley just called me. What is this nonsense?" Anne demanded.

"I'm taking a few days off."

"You can't do that! You're booked at the Civic Arena tonight and I have you on the red-eye to New York to be on *The Today Show* in the morning and Letterman tomorrow night."

"Cancel them, all of them."

Anne's tone turned to butter and sugar. "David, I'm doing this for you and the church. The ministry needs you."

"Are you, Anne? Or are you doing it for yourself? Goodbye, Anne. I'll call you in a few days."

"David, don't do this. David!"

He flipped the phone closed and dropped it on the bed. Rubbing his eyes, he stepped out onto the terrace. Bracing his hands on the railing, his eyes followed the lights blinking on all over the city. The buzzing phone skittered around on the bed. The sound reminded David of a spoiled child clamoring for attention. On the street below, cars pulled to the side as an ambulance sped by, siren blaring, lights flashing, turning the roadway blood red.

David's thoughts drifted back to the day seven-year-old Bobby fell from his tree house. As usual, David was delayed until after five at the church. Their neighbor Mr. Jenkins ran the three blocks from his home to tell David his son was being rushed to the hospital. The next day Mr. Jenkins stayed in bed, his arthritis twisting his body in knots.

In the waiting area of the emergency room, Anne clung to David, crying her eyes out. "Oh David, I'll never forgive myself. I was hanging clothes on the line, I—" She burst into loud sobs.

He held her close, smoothing her hair and kissing the top of her head. "It will be all right, honey. God will take care of him," he whispered in her ear, hoping he was right. When the doctor came looking for them, he found them deep in prayer. He waited for a few minutes, reluctant to interrupt. He had five patients to see. He cleared his throat. They didn't hear. He shuffled his feet. They didn't stir. Finally, he stepped over to David and laid his hand on his shoulder.

Stopping in mid-sentence, David jumped to his feet. Anne turned her tear-filled eyes to the physician. "How bad is it, doctor?" David asked, his hands shaking.

Dr. Jefferson smiled. "Pastor, you must have special angels watching over that little boy. There's not a scratch or bruise on him. Even better, the x-rays show nothing broken."

"Oh, thank God," Anne cried, falling to her knees and covering her face. She began to sob.

"Thank you so much, doctor," David said, gripping the smiling man's hand in both of his.

Stepping back into the suite, David grabbed the few toiletries he had unpacked and tossed them into his suitcase. He looked around the room, then snapped it closed. Dressing hastily, he slipped on heavily-tinted sunglasses and pulled his Dick Tracy fedora down over his eyebrows.

He opened the door cautiously. No one was in the hallway. Wrestling open the heavy stairwell door, he hurried down the 15 flights. A blaring alarm sounded as he pushed open the lobby door. David felt like a thief sneaking out to avoid paying his bill. As he stepped into the hallway a hand grabbed his forearm.

"Where do you think you're going?" the uniformed security officer yelled over the din.

"I was just trying to avoid any media." David spoke so meekly the guard had to read his lips.

"Oh, you that preacher, aintcha?" the guard hollered. "You come with me. I'll get you past the newshounds." Dropping David's arm, the officer closed the door, shut off the alarm and took off down the hallway. David had to jog to keep up. As the officer hurried along, he spoke in low tones into his radio. Pushing through a door marked Staff Only, he led David through the kitchen. A short, stocky man looked up from slicing a tomato into a salad.

"Preacher's trying to avoid the crowd." Holding his knife in mid-stroke, the man nodded and gawked at David. The officer opened a door at the back of the kitchen. In the alley, a cream-colored limousine idled. "Joe will take you anywhere you want," he said, gesturing to a tall black man holding open the limo's back door.

Sliding in, David studied the interior: plush velour seats, a small refrigerator, a well-stocked mini-bar with plenty of ice, garnishes and swizzle sticks. A miniature TV stared at him, its face blank. The limo paused at the corner. David jerked as the phone beside him buzzed.

"Where to, Reverend?" Joe asked.

"Where is the nearest homeless shelter, Joe?"

"Why, Mr. Reverend, you can't go there," Joe warned. Those people gonna be asleep now, and you don't want to mess with the ones that ain't."

"It'll be all right, Joe. Just take me there."

"Yes sir," Joe said with a sigh. He pulled onto the Boulevard of the Allies. David gazed out at the sidewalks. People were everywhere, walking in groups, crossing streets, stepping into restaurants and bars. Behind, in front of and on both sides of the limo, traffic moved at a fast clip.

At the beginning of his ministry, David would sit at the mall in Indianapolis for hours, just watching people rushing to and fro and praying for them. The realization that each and every one of them would spend eternity somewhere was sharp in his mind. His heart ached for the lost. Many times tears would run down his cheeks. Passersby pretended not to see the strange man sitting on the bench crying. How long it had been since he felt those stirrings of compassion.

Somewhere along the line his heart had turned to stone. The everyday business of fundraising, writing, promoting and administration had stolen his fire and left him cold and unfeeling to the spiritual needs of those around him.

"We're here, Reverend," Joe said, braking to a stop in front of the North Side Mission. He turned to look nervously at David. The three-story brick building appeared to be at least 100 years old. Chunks of broken concrete lay here and there on the steps leading to the entrance. The blackened bricks bespoke the smoky city's past; a boarded up window testified to its present. The cracked glass front door opened and a young man of college age jogged down the steps, stopping short at the sight of the limo. In this neighborhood, his dark suit, white shirt, and paisley tie made him look like he'd taken a wrong turn off the Fort Duquesne Bridge.

Joe sat quietly in his secure compartment. David opened the back door as the young man approached. "Sir, can I give you something to read, please?" His face beamed as he came closer and held the gospel tract out to David. "It will help you to know God. Money can't bring happiness, only Jesus can."

He came to a skidding halt, his loafers crunching on the broken glass that littered the cracked sidewalk. His jaw dropped. His face paled. He stuffed the tract back into his pocket. "Reverend Padgett, I… I didn't mean to say you're lost, or anything," he stammered. "I'm just handing out tracts."

"That's all right, son," David said as he started to pull the door closed. The young man grabbed the outside handle and David found himself in a tug of war. Joe anxiously watched the exchange through the side-view mirror.

"You're my hero!" the young man cried. "I want to be just like you."

"Go, get me out of here!" David shouted to Joe. The limousine shot forward, tearing the door handle out of the young minister's hand. He stood staring down at a bleeding gash in his palm, then called out, "But I just wanted to talk to you!"

David closed his eyes and leaned back. What a fool he was to think he wouldn't be recognized. "Drop me at the corner, Joe," he said, gripping the handle of his carry-on.

"You're kidding, right? Joe said, his face screwing into a frown. "You gonna get yourself killed, Preacher."

When the limo stopped at the intersection, David jumped out. The $50 bill fluttering down beside Joe went unnoticed. His attention was drawn to the fleeing man. Everything in him cried out to protect the reverend. Hurrying through an alley, David reached the next street and hailed a cab. Deepening his voice, he said, "Airport, please."

Eyeing him suspiciously, the driver replied, "Yes, sir."

Usually whenever David took a cab, the driver would engage him in conversation. This cabbie kept silent for the entire 25-mile ride, but anytime David glanced up he saw the man looking at him in the rearview mirror. As soon as they pulled up to the terminal, David tossed three bills—more than enough to cover the fare plus a generous tip—onto the front seat. Then he scooted out the door and disappeared into the building.

# Chapter 12

In her mansion on the south side of Grafton, Linda
Darby settled back against her pillow. She placed her latest
letter to the deacons on the bedside table. Maybe this time
they would listen to her and cut David's salary. It wasn't right
for any preacher to make that much money.

Her specially made king size bed, a walnut four-poster,
was imported from Ireland. The mattress supporting her
arthritic back was designed by a Swiss doctor and cost $5,000,
worth every penny. The Charlotte Thomas thousand-count
Egyptian cotton sheets came from a little shop in England.
Other wealthy people preferred to sleep on satin. Linda liked
cotton. "Those things are too slippery," she told Martha the
upstairs maid. "I may as well sleep on the floor, 'cause that's
where I'd end up." The bedside lamp gave just enough light
for reading. Linda preferred the room dim and quiet when she
read her mysteries.

After pouring a cup of hot chocolate from the Waterford
carafe, Linda scrunched down and pulled the covers up to her
neck. Feeling very comfortable and relaxed, she picked up the
new thriller by Mary Higgins Clark. Deeply engrossed in the
novel, she sipped her hot chocolate, heedless of the shadow
sneaking across the expansive east lawn. At the kitchen door,
the figure slid a credit card between the door and its frame.
Stepping quickly to the panel, he silenced the alarm.

By page 50, Linda had finished her second cup of
chocolate. Halfway through page 55, the book fell softly to her
chest as she drifted off.

Wearing surgical gloves, the dark figure slid open the
cutlery drawer. Its well-oiled rollers made no sound. Reaching
in carefully, the man picked up a butcher knife. There was no
need to test its sharpness. He could see the edge glinting in the
moonlight. Feeling his way along the walls, the man started up
the stairs.

Linda stirred groggily. "Hot chocolate at my age, you'd think I should know better," she grumbled. Now she had to use the bathroom. Sitting up, she swung her legs over the edge of the bed. Feeling around with her feet, she found her bunny fur mules and slid into them. Still muttering, she shuffled across the floor.

She knew good and well that tomorrow night she would do the same and the result would be the same. Old habits die hard, she thought. Sighing, she settled back into bed. As she reached for the light switch, she heard a crash in the hallway. Her heart leaped and raced. A lump came into her throat. She tried to swallow. After several attempts she managed to croak out, "Stanley? Is that you?" She called to the butler again, her voice breaking. Silence. "Martha?" No Martha.

She reached for the phone. It was dead. "Oh Lord, help me," she said in a shaky whisper. She hadn't called on the Lord in years. With her wealth she thought He was more in need of her than she of Him. She hoped he still remembered her.

Cell phone. Why hadn't she thought of it sooner? Another sound came from the hallway, a sort of whooshing like something heavy being dragged over the thick carpet.

Grabbing her purse from the nightstand cabinet, she hobbled to the walk-in closet and quietly closed the door. In the pitch black, stuffy enclosure, she shoved a trembling hand into the bag. Not there. She turned it upside down. The contents scattered among her expensive shoes. Dropping heavily to her knees, she ran her hands over the carpet. Then she remembered. The phone was charging on the dresser.

She cracked open the door. The circle of light from the lamp seemed smaller, dimmer. Darkness enveloped the room like a shroud. She took a step, praying the burglar wouldn't hear her. Don't faint now, old gal, she told herself. A few more steps, you're almost there.

A slight scraping at the door stopped her. The knob turned. With two more steps, she was at the dresser. Grabbing madly for it, she ripped the charger from the outlet. The cord let go, bouncing across the room and hitting the wall. To Linda it sounded like a chain dropping on sheet metal. The door opened a crack. The knife in the black-gloved fist was the first thing she saw.

Life came down to a matter of seconds. She pressed the on button. After an eternity the light flashed. With numb fingers she punched in 9-1-1. The door flew open. A man dressed in black rushed into the room. She stared shocked and incredulous into the face of her pastor. He bounded over the bed and came face-to-face with the terrified woman. The knife poised over her head looked to Linda to be the size of a sword.

"Nine-one-one, what's your emergency?"

From a distance, Linda's brain heard her mouth shouting, "You, what do you want? I'm calling the police! I've given all the money I'm going to give to the church!"

"Nine-one-one. Ma'am? Hello, ma'am?" The male dispatcher strained to keep calm. He wanted to reach through the phone and help her. "Hello! Ma'am? Can you speak to me?"

The man plunged the knife into Linda's heart with all his strength. "David Padgett," Linda gurgled into the phone.

Pressing a fingerprint from the surgical glove onto the knife handle, the man watched the life blood flow from Linda's body. Backing away, he bounded down the hallway, took the stairs two at a time and raced through the kitchen. The murderer dropped a ring on the floor. It rolled to the edge of the gas range and stopped. Outside, he listened. Sirens shrieked toward him, shredding the quiet night. Drifting into the shadows, he watched as three police cars roared up the driveway to the mansion. Crouching, the man ran bent-kneed across the back lawns. A quarter of a mile away, he peeled off the latex mask, an exact replica of the face of the most famous preacher in America.

# Chapter 13

Three days after he fled Pittsburgh, David let himself into his private entrance at the church. It was 2:45 AM. He quickly punched in the security code. In the ADT office, the computer recorded the time, date, and identity of the person entering the code. Security cameras followed David's passage to the elevator and his office.

Sitting at his desk, David swung around and faced the large window. The spray from the lake's fountain looked like gold nuggets shooting into the air. Street lamps cast misty auras of yellow light onto the walks. At the far end of the property, a spotlight illuminated the small church with its miniature hand-built spire pointing the way to heaven.

Walking to the bookcase, David selected a Bible with worn covers and dog-eared pages. He read the inscription on the fly leaf:

*To my dear son,*

*Always walk with the Lord.*

*May He bless your every effort for Him and*

*may God grant you many souls for His kingdom.*

*With all my love,*

*Mother*

Pulling out a chair from the conference table, David placed the Bible reverently on the seat. Kneeling before the chair, he began to turn the pages. For the next several moments, he read passages underlined by his godly mother. Rising to his feet, David looked around at his richly appointed office. The walls were covered with testaments to his success:

photos of him posing with world leaders, honorary doctorates, acknowledgements of his TV and radio ministries circling the globe.

He stepped back to the window and looked out again at the tiny, forgotten church. He closed his eyes. Surely God would understand and honor his supplication. "Oh, Lord, I can't give all this up. I've worked for twenty-three years to build this ministry. I'll preach on salvation more, but don't ask me to give up the organization."

He opened his eyes and saw movement. A figure in a white gown stood at the edge of the lake. Without taking his eyes off it, David bent his knees and fished the binoculars from the bottom drawer of his desk. He adjusted the focus wheels for distance. The eyepieces quavered in his trembling hands, banging against the bridge of his nose.

Ellen Ridgeway's desolate face came into focus, looking straight at him and crying out in grievance. The binoculars fell from David's shaking hands and bounced on the carpet. Picking them up, he forced himself to look again. She was gone. A loud rapping at the door startled him. Trembling with fear, he moved toward it. "Ghosts don't knock," he murmured. He turned the knob slowly and cracked open the door. He recognized the young security guard standing there knuckles up, ready to hammer again.

"Ss… Sorry, Reverend. I saw the light under your door. I didn't know you was here. Strange things have been happening tonight."

"What strange things?" David asked, his throat tightening.

"One of the guys said he saw a woman in a wedding gown by the lake. Another one saw her in the production room. I tell you, Pastor, since Mrs. Darby was murdered the whole crew is jittery." Too stunned to speak, David stared at the officer.

"Well, I better get back to my rounds," the man said. "Sorry to have disturbed you." David nodded and closed the door. He dropped into the chair behind his desk. Linda Darby dead? Not just dead, murdered. But by whom? Why?

He needed sleep. He made his way to the staff lounge and lay down on the sofa. Closing his eyes, he tried to clear his mind. He dozed fitfully, finally giving up on trying to sleep. In the men's staff bathroom, David shaved and showered, then walked down the hall in a robe. He kept a fresh suit in the office closet. Once dressed, he examined himself in the mirror. His eyes were bloodshot, his face haggard. He sat down and laid his head on the desk.

When Shirley arrived at 8:30, he was puttering with the outline of his new book. Calling her in, David asked about Linda Darby's murder. Haltingly, she gave him the details she said were all she knew. He had a feeling Shirley was being evasive.

"Do they have any suspects?" David asked, watching Shirley's eyes and body language intently.

She hesitated. How could she tell Reverend Padgett that, according to the detective, he was the chief suspect? "Oh, uh, I think there is somebody they're investigating now," Shirley stammered, her face flushing.

"Good, let's hope they find him," David said. "You know, Linda Darby was a crotchety, sour old woman. But she did have her good points."

Without replying, Shirley returned to her desk. Covering her face with her hands, she had a good cry. The day before, Grafton Police Chief Donald Price's preliminary investigation had led him to the church. He was lead investigator on the case with the state police assisting. He summoned Shirley to the conference room to grill her about David's whereabouts.

As a member of Grace Tabernacle and a friend of David's for over 20 years, Price knew in his gut his pastor was innocent. However, Don could not let his feelings prejudice the facts. Yesterday morning as Shirley stepped into the conference room, her eyes were fastened on the chief's imposing physique. At 46 years old, 6' 2" and 210 pounds, Don kept himself in top condition by running two miles a day.

"Can't expect my men to do what I won't do myself," he said in answer to why. "Besides, never know when I might have to outrun the preacher." Though the chief usually had a ready smile, his piercing brown eyes could be hard. It was said at the station house that if you had a criminal who wouldn't confess, just let the chief look at him.

Now those eyes stared at Shirley as the chief towered over her desk. "Is he in?" he asked simply

"Yes, sir, I'll buzz him for you."

"No!" Donald said more sharply than he intended. He saw she was trembling and softened his tone. "Why don't you take a short break?" With tears streaming, Shirley scurried off to the employees' lounge.

David was staring at the computer screen when Price knocked on his open door. David swung around in his chair. "Oh, hi, Donald. Isn't Shirley at her desk?" Receiving no answer, David held out his arms and quipped, "Did you come to arrest me?" It was a standing joke between the two friends.

Donald didn't laugh. "I sent her down to the staff lounge." David's smile disappeared. Donald eased his bulk into a visitor's chair and pulled a leather bound notebook from his jacket pocket. "David, I need to know where you've been for the last three days."

Perturbed, David asked, "Why? Did Anne ask you to check up on me?"

"Anne has nothing to do with my questioning your whereabouts," Don said briskly. "Do yourself a favor and answer the question."

Taken aback, David said meekly, "I was riding around on different buses."

"Buses? For three days?

"Yes!"

"Where did you eat? Where did you sleep?"

"I ate out of cans and wrappers from convenience stores and slept under the stars," David answered curtly.

"You're not the outdoor type," Donald snapped, tossing the notebook on the desk. "So you can't or won't account for your whereabouts."

David looked plaintively at the chief. "What's going on, Don? We've known each other for more than 20 years," he said, wiping his sweaty palms on his trouser legs.

"Yes," Donald said, sighing. "That's why I'm conducting this interview here rather than in the interrogation room at the station."

The door burst open and Anne charged in. Looking coldly at the chief, she yelled, "David, don't say another word!" She marched over and stood facing her husband in the narrow space between Price's knees and the desk, blocking the two men's view of each other.

"Will somebody please tell me what's going on?" David hollered.

"They suspect you, you of all people, of murdering Linda Darby," Anne said, her face white.

"You're kidding. Donald, tell me you're kidding," David said, grinning dumbly as he stood and looked back and forth from his wife to the chief. His pulse quickened as he was met with Price's wooden expression. "Donald, you know me! I led you to Christ!"

"Stop, David, please," Anne said. "Paul Levy is on his way."

"I need a lawyer? Are you arresting me, Donald?"

The police chief stood and picked up his notebook. "Wait for Paul. He's one of the best attorneys in the county. If anyone can help you, it would be him." With that he was gone.

David flopped down in his chair and took a bottle of aspirin from the drawer. "Anne, I... surely no one could believe I would ever take the life of another human being," he moaned.

Without a word, Anne picked up the remote lying on the desk. Pointing it at the TV in the bookcase, she punched the power button. The camera in the parking lot panned from

Grace Tabernacle's imposing facade to the female reporter's jabbering face. Anne turned up the volume.

"...Padgett. A grand jury will convene this afternoon. Unnamed sources tell CNN that evidence gathered at the scene includes a ring and the murder weapon, a bloody butcher knife. Padgett's fingerprints were on the knife. If found guilty, Padgett could face life in prison or the death penalty. Back to you."

Anne switched it off and turned to her husband. "Where is Ellen's ring?"

Head in hands, David said despondently, "I don't know. I suppose it's still hidden under my socks in my dresser." He felt all his strength draining out of him.

"How could your fingerprints be on that knife?" Anne pressed. David edged toward anger, then realized her tone was one of concern, not accusation.

"I don't know, Anne. I haven't been in Linda Darby's house in months. No, years."

Anne pressed two fingers to her lips and began to pace. "We need a battle plan." She pressed the intercom button on David's phone. "Shirley?" No reply. "Shirley? She must be in the lounge. I'll go get her. You call Robert and try to get ahold of the board. I'll be back."

David called Tibb Russell first.

"Mr. Russell's office," his secretary cooed.

"Hi, Beverly, this is David Padgett. Is he in?"

"Hold please," she said, without a trace of friendliness. David's face went numb. Beverly Watson's perplexing hostility toward David had vanished the day he appointed Tibb to the church board. From then on, she would always put David's calls through without hesitation. Once as he sat chatting with her while waiting to see Tibb, she casually let slip a couple of her boss's most closely guarded trade secrets.

Half a minute later, she clicked back on the line. "I'm sorry, Mr. Russell is not taking calls this morning," she stated. The phone buzzed to silence.

David held the receiver away from his ear and stared at it, not believing she hung up on him. Nervous and bewildered, he forced himself through the list of numbers. With each call, reality pricked him more sharply. Some were out of the office, others were "unavailable". On the last call, the secretary neglected to push the hold button. David heard the hasty instruction to "Tell him I'm not here." David hung up on her mid-sentence as she repeated it.

Anne came back into David's office looking disturbed. "She quit."

"Who?" David asked blankly.

"Shirley, David, your secretary! She told the front desk receptionist she couldn't lie for you."

# Chapter 14

The Grace Tabernacle staff was in panic mode. Unable to quell the whispering among their employees and the relentless phone calls from members and the press, department heads instituted full damage control procedures. The PR department attempted unsuccessfully to side-step the media with off-putting references to the ongoing investigation. The receptionist switched on the automated system and left for the day.

Reporters clustered around the back exit of Tibb Russell's office building swarmed around him as he hurried out the door. David gawked at the TV with his heart pounding as his board chairman distanced himself from him and the church. "I have no idea what is happening with Reverend Padgett," Tibb said, pushing his way through the reporters to his waiting limo.

"Aren't you the head of Grace Tabernacle's board?" a reporter from CBS Nightly News persisted as Russell ducked into the back seat.

"Not anymore, son," Tibb spouted. Closing the door, he signaled to the driver to go.

Anne insisted David use her secretary, Jane Goodley, at least until a replacement for Shirley could be found. At 10:50, Jane buzzed him. "Mr. Levy is here, Reverend Padgett."

David swallowed and licked his dry lips. "Send him in." Paul went right to work. Laying his brief case on the conference table, he spread out several documents. "How does it look, Paul?" David asked, not wanting to hear the answer.

Not wanting to give it, Levy leaned with his palms flat on the table and scanned the papers. Sighing, he looked into David's apprehensive face. "It's bad, Pastor," he said grimly. "You have no alibi. They found a ring identified as Ellen Ridgeway's in Linda Darby's kitchen. Your fingerprints were on the knife sticking out of Darby's chest."

"Paul, I am innocent. I wasn't within a hundred miles of Grafton that night," David protested, his mind spinning.

"Prove it and we're home free," Paul said.

David's face dropped. "I can't prove it," he answered with a husky sigh.

"It gets worse," Paul said, sliding into a chair.

"How could it get worse, Paul?" David snapped, his frustration rising into anger. "I'm being accused of one of the most hideous crimes known to man against a defenseless elderly woman. I can't supply any proof my whereabouts, the murderer planted Ellen's ring and my fingerprints are on the murder weapon. Now you tell me, what could be worse?"

"Chief Price told me they're also looking into Ellen Ridgeway's death. After the police went through her house, the landlord took a cat out of there and closed it up. No one's been inside since, but I understand the cops plan on having another look."

David stared into space, his mind refusing to accept what he'd just heard. When he finally spoke, his tone was vacant. "Ellen Ridgeway committed suicide. How can they blame that on me?"

"Because of the manner of her death an autopsy was performed. Over the objections of her mother, I might add." Paul's eyes searched the pastor's face. "Did you know Ellen was pregnant?"

David looked down at the table. What could he say without implicating Robert? "Is that why she killed herself?" he asked, thinking of the suicide notes he and Robert destroyed.

"The police think she was killed by her lover," Paul said. He took a deep breath. "And they say they have reason to believe that lover was you."

"Good grief, Paul, how can they think I could have anything to do with..." David's voice cracked as a wave of despair flooded his soul.

"They found your fingerprints on her headboard, the kitchen table and the back door," Levy answered. David's hands trembled; he grasped the edge of the table to steady them. Paul looked him in the eye. "David, level with me. I can't help you if you don't."

"Yes, it's true. I was in her home," David said, barely able to get the words out. "I received a note from her. She informed me of her... suicide plan."

"So you went to her house? How did you get in? Did she let you in?" Paul asked, writing on a yellow legal pad.

"No, she was dead when I got there. She had taped a key to the letter."

"Okay, great. Then all we have to do is show the letter to the police." David's face paled. "You do have the note?" Paul asked, feeling a sense of dread.

"Notes," David said.

"She left more than one?"

"Three. I... destroyed them."

"All of them?"

"Yes," David said, hoping he had.

"Why, David? Why would you do something so...?" The lawyer stopped short of calling his pastor stupid.

"I wanted to protect the church."

"Well, there's nothing we can do about it now. Perhaps the grand jury won't return an indictment," Paul said as he turned from David's gaze and shoved the legal pad into his briefcase. His cheeks were burning. He wondered if you really do go to hell for lying.

At the door, he turned and said, "I'm going to call a friend of mine from law school, Lenny Sabine. He's a great criminal attorney." He stooped over an occasional table and wrote Sabine's name and number on the back of his card. He left it there and was gone.

Five minutes later Anne and Robert came into David's office. Still sitting at the conference table, David grasped his hands together but couldn't stop the shaking. "They know I was in Ellen's house," he said, close to tears.

"How could they?" Anne asked.

"My… fingerprints were on some furniture and the door."

"David, how could you be so stupid?" Anne cried. In her mind's eye, she saw her Mercedes Roadster being towed away. She'd already had to cancel two speaking engagements.

"Do they know about me?" Robert asked quietly.

"No. I don't know. I don't think so," David mumbled, a pain shooting through his heart.

Anne started pacing, tapping her chin with her finger. "David," she said, stopping to face him across the table, "you must resign. Let Robert assume the pastorate." Seeing the stricken look on David's face, she hastily continued. "It's best for the ministry." Feeling a twinge of guilt, she repressed it.

"Yes, Dad," Robert said too eagerly. "After this blows over, you can step back in."

Looking from his wife to his son and back again, David said, "You two have it all worked out. Have you picked my gravesite, too? How about next to the little church? I can see my headstone now. `Here lies David Padgett, pastor, author, murderer.' "

Anne let out a nervous titter. "David, don't be so melodramatic," she said.

"Dad, why would you even think that? We're trying to help you," Robert said, spreading out his hands.

"Well, get this through your heads. I'm not resigning. They'll carry me out of here first. I built this church, the room you're standing in, every blessed foot of it." The intercom buzzed. David strode angrily to his desk. "Yes, Jane?" he said, trying to temper his tone.

"Mr. Russell is on your private line, sir."

"Just a minute." David pushed the hold button. "Robert, go to accounting. See where we are financially. Anne, get with PR. Call my agent in New York. See if this is hurting my book sales." Anne and Robert exchanged puzzled looks. "GO!" David shouted.

As the door closed behind them, David sank into his chair and pressed the flashing button. "Tibb, it's so good of you to call. I thought everyone had given up on me," David said, smiling through a sigh of relief. Russell's reply caused his breath to catch.

"David, I'll get right to the point. I want your resignation by end of business today."

"But… Tibb, I'm innocent."

"Maybe you are and maybe you aren't," Tibb said, biting off each word. "Doesn't make any difference. I have it on good authority that the grand jury is going to indict you. You need to step down before that happens."

"Look, Tibb, I can't give up what I've worked for all these years."

"Son, your stock's falling faster than an avalanche on Mt. Rushmore. You have no choice."

"Yes, I do," David seethed, clenching his fist. "When things were going well you couldn't wait to come on board. Now we're going through a rough time and you want to dump me. No sir."

"If you don't quit this day before sunset I'm gonna bury you!" Tibb bellowed.

"You can try!" David shouted, slamming down the phone. Leaning back in his chair, he buried his face in his hands. He felt faint. He'd skipped breakfast; his stomach wouldn't allow him to even think of lunch.

Not knowing what else to do, he retrieved the key to the secret room from its hiding place under the desk. Darkness enveloped him as he closed the door. He groped for the chair, the same hard straight-back he'd sat in while consulting with his advisors in his old house.

Many times Anne had argued in favor of replacing the atrocious thing with a comfortable, upholstered easy chair. David stubbornly refused. This chair was his connection to the past. The day he met Tibb Russell, he carried the wooden ladderback into the bathroom. He hung two towels over the curtain rod and turned off the lights. That first night he sat in the darkness, waiting. Nothing happened. For five nights, he sat in that chair, feeling foolish and a little scared, but waiting.

During the day, he devoured the books Tibb recommended. Every night, he sat in the darkness.

Six-year-old Robert missed his father. Always before they would play during the hours between supper and bedtime. Now the child would stand outside the bathroom door knocking and crying until finally becoming discouraged and wandering back to his mother.

Finally, on the eighth night, there was no disruption and David opened his mind. He cleared out all thoughts of the church, God and his family. A strange feeling overcame him, something he had never experienced. Alarm bells went off in his head, but he gritted his teeth and dismissed them.

A few minutes later, he was shocked but pleasantly surprised when Abraham Lincoln walked in. Abe sat down in a non-existent chair and smiled. After a while he spoke. "Son, what is it you want?" he asked in a low, gravelly voice.

David was sure he'd lost his mind. How could a man who died so long ago be sitting here in the darkness with him?

"Speak up, don't be afraid," Lincoln prompted. "You know, many men came to my office during the War Between the States wanting me to help them."

"I want to build a big church!" David blurted. "A really big church."

"Now, remember what Tibb told you. You have to know what you want before you can get it," Lincoln counseled.

"I want to reach a million, no, ten million people for Christ."

"Well, now you're talking. But if we do this we're going to need some help. Let me introduce you to some friends of mine."

Two men came through the darkness. David recognized them from photos in his high school sophomore history book. Thomas Edison and Andrew Carnegie stood at each side of Lincoln as a table suddenly materialized between David and the three apparitions. The ghostly figures spoke in hushed tones among themselves, discussing David's attendance problem.

96

"We must have him. He drew large audiences in his time," Edison asserted.

"I agree," Carnegie said, his brogue thicker than it was in life. David wanted to ask to whom they were referring, but kept quiet for fear of breaking the spell. Lincoln turned to him. "David, there is someone whose advice we believe will benefit you. His beliefs are certainly not your own. He will, however, be a great asset to your ministry. May we ask him in?"

Afraid to do otherwise, David nodded.

"Then open the door for him, lad," Carnegie commanded, gesturing to the door which in any world but this was the full-length mirror bolted to the wall. David stood up and grasped the knob. It squirmed in his hand. He cried out as a burning sensation seared his palm. Jerking it open, he stepped back. A man marched into the room, went to the head of the table and sat down.

"You're Robert Ingersoll, the atheist," David declared in a startled croak.

"I know who I am," Ingersoll huffed. "But who are you and why did you bring me here?"

"I would think you'd be glad to be out of hell, if only for a short time," David said. Keeping his eyes on Ingersoll, he sat down across from him. His throbbing hand distracted him. Hours later he would notice a small crescent shape burned into his right palm. The white scar it left remained through the rest of his days.

Ingersoll reared back and roared with laughter. "Hell? Hell? There is no hell. That's just a lie as is everything else in that old book you infernal preachers insist on calling the Bible."

"Now, calm your temper, Ingersoll," Carnegie scolded.

"Patience, man, patience," Edison said. "It takes patience to develop anything, whether it be a church or a light bulb."

"If you want learn patience, go through a war," Lincoln mused, stroking his beard.

David ran from the room, his rational mind refusing to accept any of this. That Sunday the church split. Half the people walked out after hearing David's announcement of Tibb Russell's appointment to the board. Tuesday night David was back in the darkened room.

# Chapter 15

David sat head in hands with his elbows on his knees as the darkness swirled around him, taking on a life of its own. His advisors never appeared, yet he could hear them.

"He's a fool and always will be," Ingersoll sneered, "believing that old book."

"It's not the book, it's the man," Carnegie chimed in, the Scottish accent muddling his words.

"I am horribly disappointed in him," Lincoln lamented.

The tears came slowly at first, then in a torrent. Even his most trusted consorts had abandoned him. The darkness bore down on David like black smoke, choking him. Disoriented, he groped for the door.

After what seemed an eternity, his fingers touched the button. Frantically, he pushed it. Nothing happened. He pounded on it with his fist. The door burst open. As it swung out into his office, several books tumbled from the bookcase onto the floor.

A strange little man sitting at the conference table jerked to the side as David stumbled through the break in the oak paneling. "Oh, goodness, there you are!" he blurted. A scarred leather briefcase lay on the table in front of him. While David's eyes adjusted to the light, he fixed them on the man and wondered if he had slipped in behind Ingersoll. The shock of carrot red hair, red bow tie, pink shirt and checked blue suit gave the man a clownishly bizarre appearance, as though he wanted people to laugh or run away when they saw him. The fact that his face was as stoic as a judge's made his persona all the more unnerving.

Rising, he held out his hand. "I'm Lonnie Sabine, Reverend Padgett," Lonnie said. Still woozy, David stuck out his hand and tried to remember where he'd heard that name.

Sabine's grip was firm and steady. The seasoned attorney shook hands with his clients for two reasons: first to introduce himself, then to gauge the emotion flowing through their bodies. If their hands were clammy and trembling, he was probably defending an innocent person. David passed with flying colors.

"Well, Reverend Padgett, shall we begin?" Lonnie asked, sitting back down in the plush chair and opening his briefcase.

"Begin?" David asked warily as he moved to a chair across from Sabine.

"Let me speak bluntly, David. May I call you David or would you prefer reverend or doctor?"

"David is fine."

"David, the grand jury will indict you this afternoon."

David crash-landed to reality. "But, but how can they? I didn't kill Mrs. Darby. I wasn't even in town."

"David you're a big fish and this is an election year," Lonnie enlightened him. "Your fingerprints were on the knife sticking out of Linda Darby's chest. A dead woman's ring was found in her kitchen. That woman worked for you here at the church. The prosecutor believes you killed her to shut her up. Word is you two had an affair."

"The prosecutor has attended Grace Tabernacle for over ten years. I counseled with him for months when he was first establishing his practice," David said, cold sweat beading on his forehead. He felt as if someone had driven a fist into his midsection.

Lonnie took a deep breath, reached into his briefcase and laid a picture on the table. A young, attractive blonde woman in a ruffled yellow dress smiled up at them. Her blue eyes sparkled, her pink cheeks spoke of health and clean living.

"Do you know this lady?" Lonnie asked, his fingers tapping the photo.

"I don't think so. I can't be sure. Is she a member of my congregation?" David asked, frowning.

"This is Susan Blankenship. She was a freshman the year you graduated from Taylor. She disappeared that April. Her body was found six weeks later in a shallow grave a mile from the campus."

"That was almost thirty years ago. What are you getting at?" David glared mistrustfully at the lawyer.

"What I'm saying, my friend," Lonnie said, twirling his fingers around his bow tie, "is—"

"Will you please stop that! I'm nervous enough as it is!" David shouted, jumping to his feet and turning away.

It took a minute for Sabine to understand. "Oh, sorry, it's become a habit. When I'm questioning a witness I run my finger over my tie and it distracts them. You'd be surprised what people will say when they're distracted."

"I am not on the witness stand nor do I intend to be," David said sharply. "And why are you dragging up a poor girl who was murdered three decades ago? Just because she was killed with a butcher knife doesn't mean I did it."

"David," Lonnie said, the expression on his face hardening. "I never said she was stabbed. How would you know that if you never knew her or anything about her?"

"Look Mr. Sabine, Lonnie, I—"

Lonnie held up his hand. "Stop! I don't want to hear your explanation. If you're guilty don't tell me. If you're innocent it doesn't make any difference."

"Do you mean my innocence is not your concern? As my attorney—"

"Sit down, David. As your attorney I will defend you to the best of my ability. However, in my mind's eye I must see you as an innocent man. The last thing I want is to have images of dead women floating through my mind as I cross examine prosecution witnesses. On the other hand, if you're not guilty the image I have of you will spur me on to a better defense."

Lonnie's cell phone rang. "Excuse me," the lawyer said, reaching into his jacket pocket. Just then David's desk phone began to ring.

"David," Anne cried, gasping with sobs.

"Calm down, Anne, what's wrong?" David said impatiently, wondering how much more he could take. Before she could tell him, there was a knock at the door.

101

Flipping his cell phone closed, Sabine said, "Prepare yourself, David. A few minutes ago the grand jury returned an indictment against you. Unless I miss my guess, the police are here to arrest you."

Anne's sobbing clicked to silence as David let the phone slip from his hand into the cradle. Lonnie opened the door to Grafton Chief of Police Donald Price.

"Don, what's going on?" David asked in a bewildered whine as he came from behind his desk.

"Pastor, I've got to take you in," Don said, his face in a grimace.

"Don, Don, you know me. You know I would never—"

Lonnie stepped aside as Price headed across the room. "David, I must counsel you to not say another word," the lawyer cautioned.

"But Don is my friend," David protested, his whine becoming more strident.

"David, at this time you don't have any friends." David's jaw dropped; he stared at the lawyer. "You cannot trust anyone. We are fighting for your life." Sabine said, following the chief to David's desk.

"Mr. Sabine is right, Pastor," Don said. "As much as I believe you couldn't murder anyone, I'm an officer of the law. If you say anything, no matter how insignificant, I must include it in my report."

David's stood in utter disbelief as his lips went dry and numb. He opened his mouth but no sound came out. Licking his lips, he tried again. "Do... do I have to be handcuffed?" he stammered, his voice barely above a whisper.

"No," Don said, laying his hand on his pastor's shoulder. A single tear ran down his right cheek. The big man didn't wipe it off. As Don led David from the opulent surroundings he would never see again, Lonnie trailed behind. As they made their way down the hall, office doors slammed shut just before they passed.

David felt humiliation and outrage burning his cheeks and tearing at his heart. He had hand-picked most of the employees of Grace Tabernacle. Some had sought him out after being fired from positions in the secular world. Many had little to recommend them. He gave them another chance even after hearing from their former employers that their job performances were mediocre at best. Now, like the rest of the world, they were turning on him like a pack of jackals.

Stepping out of the elevator, the three men walked silently through the vestibule. Everything appeared normal. Water still fell from the fountain into the koi pond; the scent of blooming roses perfumed the air. Normal, that is, until the police chief opened the door.

A crowd of security guards, police officers, reporters and curiosity-seekers milled around the parking lot. Immediately upon spotting David, reporters from broadcast and cable news networks surged forward, breaking through the police line.

"Reverend Padgett! Reverend Padgett! Are you a serial killer?" A dark-haired woman holding a microphone shouted.

"Did you murder Linda Darby?" another bellowed. "Were you aware she had changed her will?"

"I... uh," David stuttered, wanting to defend himself.

Lonnie held up his hand. "Reverend Padgett is innocent of all charges the state has leveled against him. We have no further comment at this time other than to say we are eager to be vindicated in a court of law," he said in a loud, imperious voice as he pushed his way through the crowd.

Once his client was safe in the back seat of a patrol car, Lonnie rushed to his Bentley. As Don led the line of police vehicles out of the parking lot, David twisted his head to look back at his stately mega church. They turned on Oak Street and passed Eden Park. Someone had shut off the fountain.

For the first time in years, David felt like an outsider. Tears flowed down his face as the chain link fence between him and everything he loved whizzed past. Behind them, a caravan of police and media vehicles snaked for two blocks. Inside the police cars, conversations centered on other preachers who had fallen from grace. Some spoke with sadness, others joked. David could recite their words without hearing them. How many times had he himself excoriated some preacher for allowing himself to be overcome by sin?

At the interstate entrance ramp, the patrol cars sped up. In a mortifying spectacle of flashing bubble lights and sensational reportage, David left Grafton for the last time. The prayer in his heart was one of condemnation: All these years I served you, Lord. All the times I sacrificed for you. Never again.

He plunged into the chasm he so feared. Darkness enveloped his soul.

# Chapter 16

The people of Steuben County were proud of their new security complex. The top two floors of the north building could house 200 inmates. The sheriff's office occupied the ground floor. Across the way was the Justice Center, comprised of two courtrooms, offices for the prosecutor and public defenders and the Steuben Police Department. A tunnel connected the jail to the courtrooms. Security cameras monitored every square inch of the buildings and grounds.

At 2 PM, the caravan turned into the parking lot in front of the jail. Don brought his patrol car to a halt at the main entrance. With his head down and tears streaming from his eyes, David was led up the wide front steps. Don hurried him along, trying to avoid the throng of reporters running across the lot. They almost made it.

A slightly balding man ran up the steps. Breathing hard, he shoved a microphone into David's face and shouted, "How does it feel to fall from grace, Reverend Padgett?" Sheriff's deputies and police officers lining the steps smirked. One or two of them laughed out loud. Don gave them the look for which he was so famous.

"How do you think it feels? David snarled through his sobs. His demeanor was so volatile the reporter pulled back the mike, afraid David was going to bite it. "This is the worse day of my life," David cried, his voice filled with anguish and fear.

"Just wait, you ain't seen nothin' yet," the officer holding the door for them sniped.

Don gave the man a scathing look. "How'd you like to make door opener your permanent assignment?" he snapped as the grin quickly disappeared from the officer's face.

David's introduction to lock-up was a nightmare. Like most jails in the US, Steuben County's was dangerously overcrowded. In the holding cell, David literally tripped over a burly inmate. Winding up, the man rewarded him with two black eyes and a fat lip before officers could pull him off. The next day David's booking photo was disseminated to news outlets across the country. His raccoon-ring eyes and swollen purple lip made him look like the heinous criminal he was accused of being.

Lonnie Sabine and Chief Price appeared that day via satellite on *Good Morning America* and *The Today Show*. Each one said David's beat-down was an isolated incident. Price said they were taking precautions to make sure it didn't happen again. Lonnie again assured the public of his client's innocence. Don promised to ramp up the investigation. Then they were off the air.

David knew he would be the target of many more assaults. After all, everyone including God hated him. His one phone call was to the church. Only collect calls are permitted to be made from jail.

"It's a great day at Grace Tabernacle. How may I help you?" Jenny sounded as sweet as ever.

"Will you accept a collect call from...?" The automated voice paused.

David hesitated, unsure of what to do. "Say your name, Padgett!" a nearby deputy barked.

"David... Padgett!" David shouted into the phone.

Jenny didn't miss a beat. "No, I'm sorry. I have been instructed not to accept collect calls. Have a nice day."

"Jenny, it's me, Pastor Padgett," David said, desperation heightening his pitch.

She paused, then repeated, "I'm sorry, I've been instructed not to accept collect calls." The nervousness in her voice was evident. "Have a nice day." Her tone reflected her awareness of what a ridiculous statement that was. There was a click.

Price insisted David be placed in one of the few available isolated cells. To say he spent a hellish night there would be an understatement. The pain radiating from his back to his face as he tossed fitfully on the steel bunk could not match the ache in his heart. This is crazy, it's not happening, it has to be a bad dream, he told over and over. At two in the morning the tears came again. They started as a trickle and progressed to a flood. Exhausted physically, mentally and spiritually, he finally dozed off around four.

In his dream, he, Anne and five-year-old Bobby were barricaded in the little church. Outside, an angry mob shouted obscenities at David. Suddenly he was in the huge auditorium at Grace Tabernacle. Every seat was filled and the aisles were packed with people standing. David never allowed overcrowding in his church. Nevertheless, ushers kept leading more through the open back doors.

At the podium, David was preaching on the title chapter of his latest book, *Love Unlimited*. The hordes of people piling in from every direction upset and distracted him. He turned to his son seated behind him. "Robert, we're too crowded, please take care of this before it gets out of hand." Robert simply stared at his father. "Robert, please."

Suddenly, a man halfway back stood and waved his arm. David recognized Tibb Russell. A thrill shot through the pastor's heart. Having been on the board of directors for 21 years, Russell had never attended a single service. "Everything I need spiritually I get from my dark room," Tibb would say each time David invited him.

As David opened his mouth to acknowledge his mentor, Russell shook his fist and shouted, "Murderer!" The man next to him took up the cry. Soon it spread to the entire auditorium, then to the overflow crowd outside. People screamed the hateful word. In the Sunday school rooms, teachers led the children in the chant, their arms waving as if the accusation was a popular song.

David turned to see Robert smiling. "Just confess, Dad. It will make things so much easier."

"Yes, dear," Anne said as she stepped onto the platform. She kissed him on the cheek. "Think of the ministry. Think of the finances. I want to keep my Roadster."

In a wave starting at the back of the sanctuary and working its way to the front, the congregation began stomping their feet. The noise pounded against David's ears. He covered them with his hands. A drum began to beat, keeping time with the shouting and stomping. David turned to run. Hands came out of nowhere from every direction, grabbing him and throwing him to the floor. Pain shot through his elbows and knees. His eyes popped open. He had fallen from the bunk onto the concrete floor.

As he started to climb back onto it, he noticed light shining through a hole in the door. Someone was pounding on its metal surface. "Hey, murderer, come get your breakfast. I ain't got all day." David crawled to the open portal. Lying on its vertical surface was a tray holding a plastic spoon and a Styrofoam bowl and cup.

"C'mon! I got others to feed!" the tall black man in a blue jumpsuit yelled. Realizing this was the morning meal, David pulled the tray toward him. In his haste, his shaking hand tipped the tray and the cup fell backward. He watched in horror as the lukewarm coffee sprayed onto the trustee's leg and the floor. The black man cursed loudly.

A deputy poked his head out of his office door across the way. "What's going on?" he demanded.

"He threw hot coffee all over my legs," the trustee bawled, shaking his legs as if insects were crawling on them.

"Billy, do you want to lose your job and go back into population?" the deputy threatened as he came into the hall and stood with his feet spread and his hands resting on the sides of his belt.

"But he threw coffee on me! I wouldn't lie to you, Officer Cadwell, you being a Christian and all."

Cadwell was unimpressed. "It'll be on tape, Billy. Let's go down and take a look." Cadwell knew there was no tape. In this modern age, computers captured every movement in the jail. He also knew Billy had no head for technology.

"All right let's go," Billy said, walking toward the elevator. Cadwell could never leave the floor unguarded, but he kept up the bluff and followed, hoping Billy would cave. Sure enough, halfway to the elevator Billy glanced over his shoulder, his eyes flickering with uncertainty. "I ain't got time for this," he said, wheeling around and heading back to his food cart. "I gotta feed all these men." He removed a tray. Cadwell waited until Billy pushed it through to the inmate in the cell next to David's and continued down the row.

As Billy ambled toward the next cell, Cadwell came up beside him. Pointing to the puddle on the hall floor, he ordered, "Get some paper towels and clean up that mess, and get that man another cup of coffee."

"But Officer Cadwell, if'n I do that I gotta go all the way back to the kitchen."

"Then you better get moving unless you want me to call control and have them send up another trustee," Cadwell said, stepping back through his office doorway and picking up the phone.

"I'm goin', I'm goin'," Billy said, trudging toward the elevator.

"Billy!"

"What?" Billy turned to the officer. Cadwell held up a roll of paper towels. Billy shuffled back and took it. Grumbling to himself, he bent down and swiped halfheartedly at the spilled liquid.

"Thank you," Cadwell said with a big smile.

Billy returned with a steaming cup of coffee and headed toward David's cell. "I'll take that," Cadwell said. Reluctantly, the trustee relinquished the cup and continued down the hallway, muttering as he went.

"Here's your coffee, Reverend Padgett," Cadwell said, maneuvering the cup through the cuff port.

"Thank you," David said, eyeing the man uneasily.

"My name's Jack Cadwell." The officer held out his hand. David shook it limply.

"I pastor Fairview Baptist Church just outside of Grafton."

The first thing to pop into David's mind came rushing out of his mouth. "How many in your congregation?"

"Oh, nothing like Grace Tabernacle. We're chumming a bunch, only catching about fifty." He laughed at his joke. The sound was pleasant. Wary of the minister's motive, David stifled a chuckle. He tried to remember the last time he laughed.

"I know you're going through a rough time now. Just remember, the Lord is with you every step of the way."

Bile rose in David's throat. Bitterness took root in his heart. "You're mistaken, Reverend Cadwell. When I was bringing in a million dollars for Him, He was by my side. Now that I'm in a jail cell, He's deserted me."

"Didn't you write the book, *The God of the Storm*? In it you wrote that when the tempest is the heaviest, God is the closest to your soul."

"I was wrong, is that what you want me to admit?" David snapped. "My life is a disaster and God isn't helping."

"No, I just want you to recognize the fact that He said He would never leave us or forsake us."

"Well then He lied. The fact is He has forsaken me."

"Reverend," Cadwell said, "the Bible says if we confess our sins he is—"

"Excuse me," came a pugnacious voice from behind. "Are you trying to get my client confess, Officer?" Cadwell wheeled around and looked into the unsmiling face of Lonnie Sabine.

"No, of course not. I was simply quoting a Bible verse to him."

"What is your position here, sir?" Sabine asked haughtily.

"I'm a corrections officer, but I'm also a pastor."

"And which one of those hats are you wearing right now?" Sabine asked, twirling his fingers around his bow tie.

"Right now I'm a corrections officer."

"So if Reverend Padgett were to say anything, even unwittingly, to incriminate himself, as a corrections officer you'd be required to report it."

"Technically, yes. But as I said, I'm also a minister."

110

Sabine gave Cadwell the once-over. "Reverend or Mr. or Corrections Officer Cadwell, from this point on if my client needs spiritual counseling there are several ministers on the staff of Grace Tabernacle and I dare say each one them is sufficient enough in their knowledge of the Bible not to require them to supplement their income by working as a corrections officer," he said, jutting out his bearded chin.

Cadwell's face reddened with embarrassment. David was surprised at himself. He was taking perverse pleasure in listening to the part-time pastor's upbraiding.

"Do we understand each other, sir?"

"Of course," Cadwell said. "It's not a subtle point you make."

"Now, if you will be good enough to escort my client to the interview room, I would like to confer with him." Without another word, Cadwell unlocked David's cell and walked him down to the small glassed-in room reserved for attorneys and their clients. In violation of jail regulations, he neglected to handcuff David.

"David, let me explain to you what will take place today," Sabine said as soon as they were alone. "The judge will read the charges. Then he will ask for your plea. I will of course enter a plea of not guilty for you."

Having seen courtroom dramas from *Perry Mason* to *Law and Order*, David always thought the arraignment scenes were the most boring. Not today. He wondered if he could summon the strength to stand on his own two feet.

"What about bail? Surely they can't deny me bail?" David said, hope rising in his heart. If they released him, he would hire the best private investigators money could buy.

Lonnie pursed his lips. "I spoke to the prosecutor this morning. He will fight any request for bail no matter what the amount."

"And here he's a member of Grace Tabernacle," David said with disgust.

"That's the reason why he's going to pursue your conviction so vigorously. He doesn't want to be accused of

111

favoritism," Lonnie said. "And..." The attorney drummed his fingers.

"What?" David asked. Lonnie hesitated. "Come on, Lonnie."

"Well, as a rule I can work out a plea bargain."

"No," David said, slamming his fist on the table. "I will not plead guilty to something I didn't do!"

"Well, you won't have to worry about that," Lonnie said, looking David in the eyes. "The scuttlebutt is our esteemed prosecutor wants to run for governor. This case could do it for him." Lonnie leaned back in his chair and sighed. "He's seeking the death penalty."

# Chapter 17

Arraignments are normally simple matters. An officer leads in the offender, who is sometimes chained in a line with other prisoners. After being unlocked from the group, the accused is taken handcuffed to the defense table. The judge reads the charges and asks how the accused pleads, guilty or not. If the prisoner can't afford an attorney, the judge appoints a public defender, an overworked lawyer who rarely sees his client between court appearances. Bail is requested by the defense; the prosecutor argues why it should be denied. If the judge rules in the defense's favor, bail is set. Finally the trial date is scheduled.

The inmate is returned to jail to wait for a relative or friend to post bail. Most inmates sit in their cells for months or in some cases years before going to trial. If they see their court appointed attorney once during that time it will most likely be on the day the trial begins.

David's arraignment was anything but ordinary. News vans rolled into the security complex parking lot throughout the previous night. By 6 AM, satellites were set up, cables attached and live feeds transmitted as far away as Japan.

Surrounded by deputies and wearing a bulletproof vest, at 8:45 David emerged from the jail. His eyes were blackened, his lip split and swollen, his face haggard and brutish looking under a five o'clock shadow. He bore little resemblance to the suave, debonair television evangelist.

In New York, CBS and NBC interrupted their regular programming to show live feed of David on his way to court. Don's request to bring him through the tunnel had been denied by the sheriff's department. Don was steamed, knowing there was no reason for that other than the prosecutor wanting a public display.

Supported by two deputies, David shuffled along in shackles. The men hurried him along, almost dragging him. Chief Price stepped out of the jail, futilely hoping to divert

113

some of the media attention away from the prisoner. Later that day, newspapers hit the stands with front-page photos of David and Anne in happier times superimposed over an image of Grace Tabernacle, along with one of David on his way to court. Headlines screamed:

## Padgett Pleads Not Guilty
## To Three Counts of Murder

*Good Morning America* and *The Today Show* brought on criminal and spiritual experts to explain how the fall of such a revered man of God could occur. Not to be outdone, *Court TV* made its presence known with its reporter posing the question everyone was thinking: "How many others has Padgett murdered? As it stands now, law enforcement agencies have re-opened unsolved murders cases that occurred in their jurisdictions during the times when David Padgett is known to have been there."

At Grace Tabernacle, one person was left in production, one in accounting and the associate pastors were sending out feelers. Anne was beside herself as to how to stop the bleeding. She called a staff meeting, to which no one showed up but Jane Goodley.

Anne was torn. Lonnie had urged her and Robert to be at the arraignment to show their support. As the time drew near, Robert was nowhere to be found. After searching the building, Anne stood at David's office window looking out over the grounds. She thought she saw movement in the little church. She rushed over there. As she opened the door to the small building, stale air assaulted her nose. Robert was sitting in their old pew. Coming to his side, she saw tears in his eyes. "It's my fault, Mom," he said without looking at her. "If only I hadn't cheated on May."

Sitting down beside him, Anne laid her hand on his knee. "We've all made mistakes," she said softly.

"Mistakes!" Robert cried, turning his tear-streaked face to her. "Mistakes? Mom, May's dead, Ellen Ridgeway killed herself and Dad's on trial for murder!"

"We have to keep our heads up, Robert," Anne said, "May's death was an unfortunate accident. Your father will be cleared soon, and then everything will return to normal."

"What's normal, Mom?" Robert asked, his face drawn. "Preaching something I don't believe? Trying to convince a grieving mother everything is going to be fine when she and I both know it won't? May and I were living a lie."

"What do you mean? You and May were the perfect couple, always laughing, holding hands, kissing."

"In public, yes, but at home we fought like cats and dogs," Robert said, burying his face in his hands.

Shocked, Anne decided not to press for details. "We'll make it through this, son. We're stronger than our biggest problems," Anne said, parroting one of David's trouble-taming platitudes.

"From *Timeless Love* by Reverend Padget," Robert mocked. "His words are just as empty as he is." He banged his fist down on the wooden seat as he cried out in anger and pain, "I hate him!"

"Robert! Surely you don't mean that."

"Mom, why did you stop calling me Bobby when I was seven?"

"You know the answer. Your father felt you should be known by a more mature, dignified name to help prepare you for the ministry."

"No one ever asked me if I wanted to be a minister. You and Dad just took it for granted that I would follow in his footsteps."

"It's a very honorable profession. Your grandfather was a pastor, as was his father."

"It may have been right for them, but not for me. I've tendered my resignation."

"Oh, Robert, no! We need you here."

Leaping to his feet, Robert headed for the door. "No you don't, Mother. Remember, 'our difficulties are just opportunities in disguise'." He stalked out of the building and strode briskly across the lawn.

Squeezing out from between the pews, Anne started to run after her son. Just inside the door, she caught her heel on the threadbare carpet runner and fell to her knees. Grasping the door handle to support herself, she waved with her free hand at Robert's retreating back. "Robert! Robert," she cried. He kept going. She collapsed in a heap on the dusty rug and dissolved in tears. "Please come back. The church needs you. I need you."

As Anne walked slowly back to the church, she saw that Robert's car was gone. Robert was gone. She called his cell phone. No answer. She waited 15 minutes and called his house phone. Nothing. Anne felt fearful and very alone. There was no one to lean on. Three quarters of the church staff had quit, the rest were looking to.

Anne found solace in her one true friend, Jane Goodley. Jane greeted her with a sympathetic smile and said, "You have a call from Rose Turner out of Atlanta."

"I'll take it in my office," Anne said, sniffling and avoiding Jane's eyes. She sat at her desk, wiped her eyes with a tissue, smoothed her hair and, forcing herself to smile, picked up the phone. "Sister Turner, it's wonderful of you to call."

"I'll get right to the point, Mrs. Padgett," Sister Turner said. Her voice had all the friendliness of a rattlesnake's hiss. "We have received thousands of requests for refunds from your appearance here. Also, the media is hounding us to death."

Anne's smile wavered and died. "It's all just a huge misunderstanding, Rose. I believe—"

"I don't care what you believe," Sister Turner snapped, practically biting off Anne's ear through the phone. "We demand you return the honorarium." Anne could hear the old woman's dentures clicking.

116

"What? Now wait a minute. You can't expect me to return the full twelve thousand. I fulfilled my obligation."

"If you read the contract thoroughly you will see we require our speakers to abstain from any appearance of evil."

Anne held the receiver away from her ear and stared at it incredulously. Her temper was rising. "As I said, I fulfilled my obligation. My husband is one of the most respected men in the country, and he will be exonerated," she answered firmly. "Besides, it was I who spoke at your conference, not him. Why should I be punished for my husband's alleged behavior? And whatever happened to innocent until proven guilty?"

"Do you normally consume a full bottle of alcohol in one night, Mrs. Padgett?" Rose asked, dragging out the word Mrs.

The blood drained from Anne's face. A Bible verse nudged the edge of her subconscious: Be sure your sin will find you out.

"Of course not. How dare you even say such a thing!"

"What about stealing? Is that standard procedure for you?" Rose goaded. The clicking sounded like castanets. The sound was driving Anne mad. She wanted to shout, Well, Poligrip is obviously not standard procedure for you!

"I have never stolen anything in my life," Anne said through her clamped jaw. "This conversation is over."

"Did you think you could steal a bottle of champagne from the limousine, hide it in your hotel room and get away with it?" Rose asked. Her teeth came down with a loud snap. It sounded to Anne like the door closing on her speaking ministry. She opened her mouth but was out of words.

"Twelve thousand dollars in my hand by the end of the week, or the news media will learn of your dirty little secret," Sister Turner said. The teeth gave a final clack before the phone hummed in Anne's ear.

Burying her head in her hands, Anne gave in to a good long cry. Her husband was in jail for murder. Her son was gone. Her speaking commission was gone. If she didn't come up with $12,000 she would be labeled a thief and an alcoholic.

When she ran out of tears, she straightened up and called Accounting. A few minutes later Harvey Lee stepped into her office. Motioning him to a chair, Anne said, "I want you to cut a check payable to Women's Rejoice in Atlanta. I have the amount and address right here." She held out a slip of paper.

Harvey looked at it. Anne gazed curiously at the sweat forming on his forehead. "I'm sorry, Mrs. Padgett, I can't," Harvey said, keeping his eyes on the paper.

"Of course you can. I have the authority to sign checks up to twenty-five thousand," Anne argued.

"Not anymore," Harvey said. His fingers twitched. Sweat ran down the middle of his back. He studied the toes of his shoes. Her shout made him jump.

"What!"

"Mr. Russell came by my office this morning."

"Tibb Russell was here? Why didn't he come to see me?"

Harvey took a deep breath. In a staccato, declarative tone similar to a town crier's, he announced: "As chairman of the board of Grace Tabernacle, Mr. Russell has frozen all accounts for Reverend and Mrs. Padgett." He took another breath. "I mean you and Pastor David. Personal and ministry."

Anne's life melted away before her eyes. Her voice was weak and faltering. "He can't do that. He has no authority over my personal accounts."

"I'm afraid he can. The church constitution gives the board compete control if for any reason the pastor is unable to fulfill his duties." After a brief moment, he added, "Or at the board's discretion."

"But, Robert will assume David's position as pastor," Anne said, hoping against hope.

Grimacing as though he'd been punched in the stomach, Harvey said quietly, "The board has dismissed you, your husband and your son from Grace Tabernacle."

"What are you talking about?" she shrieked. "David built this church! This is our home. Where is that coward Russell? Why didn't tell me this himself?"

118

Harvey stood and began backing toward the door. "I don't know. I'm just the messenger." His hands searched behind him for the doorknob. Finding it, he darted out, leaving the door open.

"Jane!" Anne shouted. Jane appeared at the door. "Thank God you're still here," Anne said. "Get Tibb Russell on the phone."

Two minutes later Jane buzzed her. "Mr. Russell is unavailable."

"What a surprise, that cowardly rat." Unaccustomed to hearing her boss speak in such a manner, Jane was silent. "You tell whoever answers that phone that I insist on speaking to him. If he refuses, I will go to the media and do everything in my power to drag his name through the mud."

Jane nervously repeated her boss's words to Russell's secretary. Three minutes later Anne's private line buzzed.

"Let me explain something to you, Anne," Russell said without introduction. "If you are foolish enough to fight me in the court of public opinion, I'll win. I always do."

"Tibb, why are you ruining us? David is your friend."

"David is an opportunist. He saw a way to pursue his dream and used me to that end."

"Why did you freeze our accounts?"

"To protect the church."

"You don't even attend services."

# Chapter 18

Russell laughed. "That's hardly the point. I have a vested interest in Grace Tabernacle. If it defaults on its loans, and there's a good chance it will, well, that property will make a wonderful headquarters for Forever Well insurance."

Anne's mouth flew open. She squeezed the receiver until it threatened to crack in her hand as the room swirled before her eyes.

Tibb Russell had just gotten started schooling the pastor's wife. "I've waited for a return on my investment for years while you and David built your little kingdom. Who do you think financed it? Who do you think persuaded the Grafton zoning board to let you construct that albatross of a church?"

Anne was close to hyperventilating. "You... can't do this," she cried, her sobs choking her words.

"Oh, yes I can, I absolutely can." He was enjoying this. "But I'll be kind. I'll give you thirty days to vacate my new home."

"New... new... home?"

"The mansion, Anne."

There was silence as Anne's dizzied mind tried to digest his statement. "Please, please don't do this. I have nowhere to go," she sobbed.

"That's not my concern. Thirty days from today I'll be moving in. If you're not out I'll have your belongings put in storage for six months. And Anne, if you mention this conversation to the media, I'll deny every word." The line went dead.

Too drained and upset to finish the day, Anne stepped out the side door marked Padgett Family Only, pulled it closed and inserted her key to lock it. It wouldn't turn. She tried again with the same result.

"I'm sorry, ma'am, this door is reserved for use by the pastor and his family," a security officer said as he walked up behind her. She turned to face him. The officer was shocked at her appearance. Her tear-stained face drooped with sadness and defeat below her squinty, red-rimmed eyes.

"Oh, Mrs. Padgett, I'm sorry, I didn't recognize you from the back."

"John, my key doesn't seem to work," Anne told him, her voice thin and raspy.

"Here, let me try mine," John Colter said, stepping in front of her. He locked the door with the new key Maintenance had given him just a couple of hours before.

"Thank you, John," Anne said with a weak smile. "This has been a terrible day."

Looking past her, Colter eyes were trained on something in the distance. "Let me walk you to… uh… home." Anne looked at him quizzically. "Some of the media people managed to sneak past Officer Waters at the entrance to the park," he explained.

"Waters? I don't believe I know him."

"New guy, only been with us a few days."

Halfway to the mansion, a man stepped out from behind a large oak tree. Startled, Anne glanced at him and lost her balance. She tripped just as he snapped the picture. As she fell, the high heel broke off her right shoe. More roughly than he intended, Colter jerked her to her feet. She screamed in surprise and pain. The officer pulled her along by the arm as she limped alongside trying to keep up.

At the curved wrought iron gate at the foot of the mansion's driveway, Colter produced another key. She followed him through. They both looked up. The loud, metallic chop-chopping of a helicopter came at them from the direction of the church. They rushed across the lawn as it hovered overhead. The logo on the side read "Channel 8 News." A man leaned out and pointed a video camera at them.

As Colter let her into the house, Anne stood catching her breath, then remembered. "Oh, my car. I left it in the parking lot. It's the blue Mercedes."

"Give me the key. I'll have someone bring it to you later," Colter said. He looked up and pointed. "After we get rid of these guys." He hurried off the same way they came.

The house was strangely still and empty. Anne called out to the maid, then the cook, but got no answer. She looked at her watch: 3:50. Their workday ended at 4:30. Maybe they had abandoned her too.

Wandering through the rooms, Anne tried to conjure one pleasant memory of living in this house. It wasn't a home, it was a fashion statement, a symbol of her husband's success. She had to reach back to the days when she, David and Bobby shared the little shack to find anything worthwhile remembering. The days when they had worked together to get...here. Anne's lips curled in bitter irony. The tears began again as her heart broke over her family, and her life, being taken down piece by piece.

The phone rang. Anne wanted to ignore it. The ringing hammered in her ears. The caller ID screen said Lane Liston. Why would he be calling?

Ten years earlier, Lane, a pastor of a small country church west of Grafton, was at odds with the IRS. Several local pastors stood with him, testifying in court or just being there for support. Lane was ultimately convicted of tax evasion and fraud, though the evidence against him was thin. Nevertheless, he did time in federal prison.

Asked by an *Indianapolis Star* reporter for his comment on the whole affair, David tore Lane Liston apart. "Among the chosen men of God there have always been a few thieves and liars," David said. "Lane is a wolf in sheep's clothing."

The same reporter asked Lane for his opinion of David. Lane stated, "Dr. Padgett is a great minister. I admire him for his wonderful accomplishments in Grafton and throughout the world."

Hoping to add some spice to his story, the reporter pressed. "Aren't you angry with him for his remarks concerning you?"

"No, no," Lane replied earnestly. "Christ never became upset with Peter and look at all he accomplished on the day of Pentecost."

On the ninth ring, Anne lifted the handset. "Hello?" she said apprehensively.

"Sister Padgett? This is Lane Liston,"

"What can I do for you, Reverend Liston?" Anne replied, surprised at the rudeness of her tone.

"You're hurting, aren't you, sister? I just wanted to assure you that we care and our prayers are with you."

"Thank you," Anne said contritely. She began to relax in spite of herself. She felt something stir in her heart that she had not experienced in a very long time.

"Is there anything you need?" Lane asked quietly.

Tears flowed freely down Anne's cheeks as her composure began to slip. "Maybe a place to stay," she said, trying to steady her voice.

Before she could stop herself, Anne was telling Lane everything. When she finally wound down, he was momentarily silent. Finally, he said, "Mrs. Padgett, you may not feel comfortable with what I'm going to suggest." Anne gripped the phone, not knowing what to expect. "I don't have the best reputation among some ministers. To this day some believe I'm a tax cheat, even though it's common knowledge that I was railroaded. But some still want to call me a shyster and deceiver."

"David doesn't think that," Anne said, lying like a schoolgirl caught stealing candy. She knew that was exactly what David believed.

"Well, I appreciate that. As you know, our church is in the country, so it might be inconvenient for you. But I've spoken to our congregation and they want to help you and your husband." He was interrupted by laughing children. "Just a moment, please." Anne heard Lane speak gently as he sent them to play in another room. He came back on the line. "What I'm saying, Mrs. Padgett, is we have a prophet's chamber at the back of our church. It would be a quiet, private place for you to stay. My people and I want you to know you're welcome to stay here as long as you need."

Anne broke down. She could not believe this man of God would be so generous, so forgiving. She managed to compose herself enough to say "Thank you." Lane promised to call her back in the next few days to make arrangements for the move.

Anne went upstairs and took a long shower. She stood under the soothing warm water and tried to close her mind to her heartaches. She let herself be carried off to a happier place.

David was back. No matter what happened in his absence, even after the repercussions of her drunken night in Atlanta, she still thought the title of her book was apropos. Perhaps his new book, "Flying with Angels", and hers, "In the Shadow of Greatness", would be released at the same time. They could host dual signings. She visualized David taking back his leadership of the church and Robert remarried and taking his rightful place working beside them.

The bubble burst the instant she shut off the water. She stepped out of the shower and back into reality. She saw her husband languishing in a prison cell, Robert lost in a wilderness and herself wandering the streets begging for money. Wrapping herself in a towel, she sat on the bed and closed her eyes, trying to recapture the fantasy. "Everything will be all right," she heard David say as he left the courthouse a free man. Robert is on his way home. Rose Turner will call any minute to apologize. Our book sales will soar because of the trials we endure!

Her eyes fluttered open. She sat there blinking as a voice within her screamed, "Lies! Lies! All lies. David will be convicted. He'll be put to death in the electric chair. Robert is lost to you forever. People will laugh at you and shun you. Your life is over, ruined, destroyed!"

"No! No!" she cried, sliding off the bed to her knees. She whimpered like a child wandering lost in the woods. She got up and began screaming, "God how could you do this to us? We served you all of our lives! David and I gave our lives for you! We dedicated our only child to you." She flopped onto the bed and sobbed into the pillow until she fell into a troubled sleep.

Dreams of goodness and nightmares of evil collided in her mind all night. She awoke disoriented and soaked in sweat. Sunlight streamed through the windows. Her pounding head hurt worse than the hangover headache she'd had in Atlanta. Throwing off the clammy towel, she stepped to the walk-in closet.

Standing nude in the doorway, she surveyed the dresses and pantsuits. What does one wear to one's husband's arraignment? Suddenly the bedroom door opened and a man in a gray uniform stepped in. For a second or two they stared at each other. At six foot, the man's bushy beard and thick eyebrows gave him a beastly appearance. "Get out of here! What are you doing in my house?" Anne screamed. She jerked a blue silk dress off a hanger, ripping the neckline almost to the waist. She held it in front of her.

The man's face blazed bright red as he turned it away. "I... I'm sorry, ma'am, I was told the house was empty," he stammered. "They said no one was supposed to be here."

"What are you doing here?" How'd you get in?" Anne demanded, her hands shaking. The movement transferred to the dress, causing it to shimmer.

"We was gettin' the house ready for the new owner, ma'am," the man said as he looked up at the ceiling. "We had to get here early, the painters are comin' in a little while."

"Get out of here. Go stand in the hall, and close that door!" Anne shouted. As he complied, Anne threw the dress over her head. She called after him, "You have the wrong house. This house belongs to the church. Who let you in, anyway?" Holding the torn neck of the dress closed, she yanked open the door and advanced on the man.

"The new owner, he let us in, ma'am," the man said, backing toward the stairs.

"Where is he, this so-called new owner?" Anne yelled, following the man down the hall. "You get him right now. Do you hear me? I'll get to the bottom of this."

Teetering at the edge of the stairs, the man called down, "Mr. Russell, they's a lady up here says we uns got the wrong house."

Stepping to the bottom of the stairway, Tibb Russell grinned up at Anne. "It's all right, Toby. I'll handle it," he said.

"Yes sir," the man said, fairly running down the stairs.

"You, you vulture," Anne hissed, her face aflame with embarrassment and anger, her eyes boring into the billionaire. "You said I had thirty days."

"Change of plans," Russell said with a chuckle. "I made an offer the board couldn't refuse."

Terror shot through Anne's heart. "What are you saying?"

"What I'm saying, Anne," Russell said as he slowly mounted the stairs to the top, "is the church is in dire financial straits. The board saw the writing on the wall and accepted my offer on this house."

"This HOUSE? This is my home! David built this ministry single-handedly."

"People are like cattle, they follow the best leader, yet they stampede at the slightest disturbance. The people of Grace Tabernacle are stampeding." Tibb caressed the highly-polished curved end of the cherry banister. "You're right, David built the church. But I built David. I transformed a sniveling, cowardly little country boy into a famous leader capable of constructing my future empire."

Russell's smarmy smile made Anne's skin crawl. Fearing she would drop, she let go of the torn fabric and braced her palms against the wall. Looking down at the floor, she pursed her lips and shook her head slowly.

"Oh, yes," Russell said, grinning. "One thing you have to understand, Anne. I'm a patient man. I will get what I want, however long it takes. And this home can still be yours."

"What? What do you mean? How?"

Russell took a couple of steps toward her. 'Marry me."

Robert could not run fast enough or far enough away from Grafton. He felt betrayed by his parents for insisting he enter the ministry and by the people of Grace Tabernacle for turning against his father. But most of all he felt deceived by God. His life was a despicable lie. Two women were dead because of him. Even if he wanted to take the helm of Grace, the board would never allow it. The name Padgett had become death to any ministry.

He passed through St. Louis at 5:15 The Interstate loop was bumper-to-bumper with city workers heading home. As he sat in traffic, he thought about May and the day he proposed to her. He was so happy, so proud when she said yes. They walked arm-in-arm back through the park, chattering excitedly about their future.

The only point of conflict was that May wanted to start their family as soon as they were married. Robert thought it best to wait a few years until his ministry was solidly established. Every few months May would broach the subject, but Robert's response was always the same. Each time he dashed her dream she would be crushed, both by what she saw as his unreasonable stubbornness and the fact that he was blind to her pain. By the end of the first year, a wedge had been driven in their marriage.

Forced to sit idle among the honking and fumes, the memory of his wife's misery came back to haunt him. He was trapped with the guilt and regret. Never before had it occurred to him how horrible it must have been for May to learn of Ellen's pregnancy.

He felt like a coward abandoning his mother and father. Yet how many times had they forsaken him for church activities? When Robert was 15, he won the lead in the school play. He studied the role of Romeo for weeks. May would play Juliet. David and Anne promised to be there.

"Wild horses couldn't keep us away," David assured him.

127

"You're going to look so handsome," Anne gushed, patting him on the shoulder.

He grinned, hoping this time they meant it. Throughout his childhood and adolescence, softball and basketball games, even birthdays parties came and went in their absence.

The night of the play as he waited backstage, he kept peeking through a crack in the curtain. His parents were nowhere to be seen. He missed his cue twice. Mrs. Walls finally came looking for him as the audience began to buzz.

"Robert, don't be frightened," she coaxed, trying to hide her impatience. "Everyone gets stage fright at times. You'll be fine."

As it turned out, he was better than fine, handing in the most lauded performance in the high school's history. Later, his parents apologized. "I'm so sorry, son," his father said. "Mr. Russell set up a last-minute meeting with the City Council and the zoning board."

Anne was all smiles telling Robert how wonderful everyone said his performance was. "And they're going to let us build the tabernacle," she added with an even bigger smile. "Isn't that terrific?"

Robert forced a smile. "Great, that's great."

"Tell him the best part, David," Anne said, looking back and forth between the two of them.

Unrolling a set of blueprints on the table, David pointed to a third-floor grid and said, "Look at this son. This is where your office will be."

As he inched along with the traffic, tears moistened Robert's eyes. He missed his parents, but he had missed them for years. First his father, then his mom.

The grand opening of Grace Tabernacle was held on Robert's 17th birthday. By the middle of the day, he was sick of people telling him what a wonderful birthday gift it was.

A free banquet was served in the Upper Room restaurant. Sneaking in through the back door, Robert filled two plates. Dodging from tree to statue to tree, he made his way to the old church. Pulling off the disappearing act made

128

him feel quite independent and self-satisfied. He knew his parents wouldn't like it. That was okay. He'd always been the good boy. Now he was going to start being his own man. He sat in the dimness of his father's tiny former office, wolfed down the food, belched loudly, snickered and watched out the back window to see if anyone was coming. If they did, he dove into the supply closest.

As the celebration wound down around three, Robert stole across the lawns to the enormous new house. Most teenagers would give their eye teeth to have their own room in a brand new mansion. Robert just wanted go home.

Outside of St. Louis, Robert almost missed the exit for Interstate 40. Halfway across Missouri, it started misting, turned to rain, then poured down in a deluge. Opening the window, he breathed in the fresh scent of God's cleansing the earth. The downpour on his arm and shoulder cooled his body. It splashed in his face and mixed with his tears. After a couple of miles, the windshield wipers couldn't keep up with it.

Pulling off at the next exit, Robert parked in the lot of a small motel. It was past nine. He had considered going on into Oklahoma. He was exhausted, his nerves were shot—he would never make it. He took a pair of dark glasses from the glove compartment and pushed them onto his face. Pulling up his collar and holding his umbrella low over his head, he dashed to the office.

A scruffy man of about 25 was sprawled in a recliner behind the counter. His loud snoring whistled through his nose. Robert hit the bell; the sound echoed through the silent room. The man stirred, turned slightly and kept on snoring. Peeved, Robert said loudly, "Excuse me." More snoring. "Excuse me!" he yelled. More snoring and a snort. Disgusted, Robert pulled on the man's foot. He came awake instantly, his feet hitting the floor. He jumped up, doubling his hands into fists. Robert stepped back, ready to run.

"Whaddaya want?" the man yelled.

Robert glanced into the back room. If someone was sleeping in there, they wouldn't be for long. "I asked you what you want," the man said again, reaching under the counter.

"A room," Robert croaked, "a room for the night."

Relaxing, the man changed his tune. "Sorry, but there's been some motels robbed around here lately. Man comes in late at night and holds up the clerk. He shot the last guy over in Clarksville."

"Just looking for a room," Robert mumbled. "Started falling asleep on the interstate."

"Well, now, we can fix you right up," the clerk said, turning around the register." You want a room in front or back?"

Robert thought quickly. "Back."

"Okay, just sign. We got one for you away from the noise. Room 107." Robert hesitated with the pen poised above the book. "Something wrong?" the clerk asked, eyeing him suspiciously.

"It's just, well, my ex-wife is stalking me," Robert said, his palms sweating. He wasn't a good liar, but he thought that sounded convincing. "She even hired a detective. I can't live with the woman." He kept his eyes lowered, remembering that the eyes are the window to the soul.

The clerk grinned, "Don't worry buddy, I got your back," he said, closing the book and shoving it under the counter. "Just fill out this little card and nobody will be the wiser."

Robert nodded and smiled while he thought for a moment. *Robert Kincaid*, he wrote, *1223 Oak St., St. Johns, Indiana*. Taking the card, the clerk scrutinized it while Robert fought the urge to grab it out of his hand and rip it up. The man pulled out a tin box half full of similar cards, placed Robert's inside and stuck the box back under the counter.

"Okay, Jack," the man said with a wink, "your secret is safe with me."

"Thank you, Mr..."

"Jimmy, just call me Jimmy, Jack."

130

Robert drove around to the back and carried in his suitcase. The room may or may not have been cleaned in the last week. Pulling some toilet paper from the roll in the bathroom, Robert did a little impromptu dusting. After shaking out the blankets and sheets, he lay fully clothed on the bed. He was exhausted; therefore, he should be able to sleep, right? Wrong! His mind was spinning. His father was in jail. According to the radio news, he and his parents had been banished from the very church they built. His wife was dead. He saw little hope.

As he closed his eyes, May's face swam in the darkness. "May, oh May, I'm so sorry. I love you," he moaned, tears trickling from his eyes.

Early in his teenage years, Robert trained himself to be unfeeling. That way he could never be hurt. He built a wall around his heart. For a short period, he allowed May to penetrate that wall. Eventually, even the small opening he allowed her closed. When they fought, she often accused him of being distant and uncaring.

He couldn't make amends with May now. He wished to God he could. However, he could prove Ellen Ridgeway committed suicide. He had hidden one of her suicide notes in his home. He determined in his heart to go back. Suddenly he felt more awake than ever before.

Grabbing his suitcase, Robert hurried to the car. As he placed the bag in the trunk, he heard three small explosions from the direction of the office. Against his better judgment, he ran toward the front of the building. He rounded the corner in time to see a small, dark car exit the parking lot. Through the driver's side window he glimpsed a bearded man pulling off a ski mask. Entering the office, he found Jimmy moaning on the floor in a pool of blood. Robert knelt beside him and pressed on the two bullet wounds in his chest, trying to stem the flow.

"Jimmy, Jimmy can you hear me?" Robert cried. A small caliber pistol lay on the floor beside the dying man. Hearing a noise behind him, Robert snatched it and jumped to his feet.

131

Swinging around on his heel, he pointed the pistol into the startled face of an elderly man in a bathrobe.

"Don't shoot!" the man screamed. Throwing his hands in the air, he nearly fell backwards through the doorway.

"No, no, I didn't shoot him!" Robert cried, suddenly aware of stickiness on his fingers. Looking down, he saw that the pistol was covered with blood. Tossing it down, he chased after the elderly man. Hearing his footsteps, the man stumbled as he ran across the parking lot.

"Call the police! He killed the clerk!" he shouted.

Chapter 19


One by one lights blinked on in the rooms. Panic enveloped Robert like a wet blanket. Detouring into the shadows, he sprinted back to the car. Leaving the headlights off, he exited through the back of the parking lot. When there was only darkness behind him, he switched on the high beams. Driving along the access road, he saw two state police cars racing in the opposite direction on the highway.

Taking a left, then a right, then another left, Robert sped down country roads. His heart hammered, sweat poured down his back. Fear made his blood run cold. The old man was going to tell the police he shot the clerk. They would never believe him. His prints were on the gun. How could he have been so stupid?

He pounded the steering wheel; the car veered to the side of the road. Soft mud caught the tire. The wheel pulled hard to the left, throwing off his hand. Before he could grab the wheel, the car careened into a deep ditch. Wearing no seat belt, Robert's head hit the dash. He saw a flash of light before he slumped unconscious onto the wheel.

Sheriff Bud Rash was exhausted and irritated. Jimmy Ward had been a thorn in his side and a nuisance to the small community for years. Marijuana was Jimmy's drug of choice and growing it in the cornfields of unsuspecting farmers in the area gave him special joy. If he could outsmart Bud, it just added some sick pleasure to his miserable life.

Now that his nemesis was dead, Bud felt an odd sense of loss. Not for Jimmy, but for the fact that his ongoing investigation of Jimmy's pot-growing enterprise would no longer fill his idle hours. Yet with Jimmy's death, the sheriff gained crystal clear evidence of the Check-In Robber's identity. The press had already redubbed him the Check-In Killer.

The bloody prints on the gun were as distinct as if they had been pressed in ink. The elderly man's checkered description of the gunman unnerved Rash a bit, but not enough to deter him. When the cops arrived at the motel, they saw a white rectangle in Jimmy's hand. It took two deputies and the sheriff to pry the register card in one piece from Jimmy's dead fingers.

"Robert Kincaid. No doubt that's an alias," Bud said, holding the card by its edges. "Check the dbase and have this dusted for prints." He dropped the card into a plastic ziplock bag and handed it to one of his deputies. "CSI here yet?"

"Yeah," the man said. "They're going over the room."

"Okay, listen, we got less than twenty four hours before he strikes again," Bud said. "Let's move on this, guy. I want Mr. Robert Kincaid in my jail by morning, if not before."

David's horror tore through him like a flaming arrow. Camera lights blazed in a glaring, hellish circle, almost blinding him. Microphones from every direction were shoved in his face, one of them bashing his jaw. The horde of scuffling reporters baited him with suggestive questions he wouldn't answer even if he could. Handcuffed, head bowed and shackled, David shuffled into the courtroom surrounded by 10 officers. Once inside, they removed the shackles but left the handcuffs in place. Pulling out a chair at the defense table, a hulking deputy shoved him into it.

"Don't worry, preacher, we'll wait for you. This won't take long," he said, smirking at David. A few of the officers laughed jeeringly.

Frowning, Lonnie Sabine turned to his client. "I'm afraid I have some bad news, David," he said in a low voice.

"I don't think I can take much more," David said, wondering what could be worse than facing three counts of murder.

"The church board has frozen your bank accounts, both personal and ministerial." David stared open-mouthed at the lawyer. "To put it bluntly, you're as poor as the proverbial church mouse and I don't work for free."

Finding his voice, David said, "You're quitting?"

Lonnie looked down and pushed a few papers around the tabletop. "I'll help you through the arraignment. The court will appoint an attorney to handle your case."

"But… but I need you."

"I'm very sorry David, you can't afford me."

"I'll find the money somewhere. I—"

"All rise! The District Court of Steuben County is now in session. The Honorable Albert Ward presiding."

"David Lee Padgett," the judge called, scrutinizing David. "Good name for a statesman or a serial killer. Which one are you?"

Without batting an eye, Lonnie Sabine stood and said loudly, "Not guilty, Your Honor!"

"So ordered. A plea of not guilty is entered. Does your client have the audacity to ask for bail?"

"We do, Your Honor," Lonnie answered firmly.

"Mr. Hargrove, what say ye?" the judge asked, peering over his glasses at the Steuben County prosecutor.

"The people request remand, Your Honor," Hargrove said in his most authoritative voice.

"I should hope so," the judge said. "Pray tell, why would the people object to this fine upstanding gentleman walking the streets of our fair city?"

"Well, Your Honor, I suppose I just have a soft spot for the women of Steuben County and would like to see them enjoy another day of life."

"I couldn't agree more. Bail is denied," the judge declared, bringing down his gavel with a bang. "Anything else, gentlemen?" His Honor looked intently at the two men at the defense table.

Clearing his throat and twirling his bow tie, Lonnie said, "Well, Your Honor, it seems the church board has frozen Reverend Padgett's assets."

"Hmm. So they believe your client to be a thief in addition to his other endeavors?" the judge said, grinning.

Enough was enough. David jumped to his feet, his handcuffs rattling. "Excuse me, sir. I am neither a murderer nor a thief!" he exclaimed. "I'm being framed and I demand this court release me immediately!"

Glaring harshly at David and Sabine, the judge banged his gavel as if he were hammering a nail. "Counselor, control your client or I will cite you both for contempt!"

# Chapter 20

Grasping the back of David's jumpsuit, Lonnie yanked him down into his chair. "I apologize, Your Honor. The fact is, however, Reverend Padgett is no longer represented by my firm."

"Oh, and why is that?" His Honor asked.

"As I mentioned, he is indigent."

"Very well, I'll appoint an attorney. Bailiff, call in Mr. Cash Barlow. I believe I saw him skulking in the hallway."

"This is a farce," David said loudly enough for the judge to hear. The judge eyed him. The prosecutor chuckled.

"I'm so glad I can provide entertainment for you," David snipped across the aisle.

The prosecutor smiled, looked straight ahead and said, "This is one trial I'm going to enjoy."

"Please refrain from speaking, Reverend," Sabine cautioned, placing a restraining hand on David's shoulder.

The courtroom door opened and the bailiff came in with a doe-faced young man. "What is he, sixteen?" David huffed. "He can't be my attorney. I won't allow it."

Gathering up his papers and shoving them into his briefcase, Sabine said, "Good luck, Reverend Padgett." Standing to his feet, he made a quick exit.

Cash Barlow nervously approached the defense table and gave David a timid "Hello."

"Mr. Barlow, it's a joy to see you in my courtroom," the judge said with a Cheshire cat smile. "You know our friendly neighborhood prosecutor, and this gentleman is your client, the Reverend Doctor Mr. Padgett."

Feeling a bit more confident, Barlow grinned. "Th... thank you, Your Honor." He extended his hand to David, who ignored it and stared straight ahead. Clamping his hand around David's arm, the officer led him away. As David was returned to his cell, the inmates taunted him.

"Hey, preacher, thought you was a-leavin' us."

"Naw, he can't tear himself away." Snickers and guffaws erupted from the cells.

"Hey, Reverend Padgett, you gonna preach us a sermon?"

"Knock it off," the officer yelled, only to be met with giggling and outright laughter. As the steel door closed, David pushed his hands through the opening. After removing the handcuffs, the officer slammed the cuff port door shut.

Alone in the bleakness, David sat on the bunk and massaged his wrists. Hopelessness ate through his heart. He hadn't even seen Anne and Robert before the judge closed the courtroom to the public. They had abandoned him. He would die alone in some stinking hole on death row. They had all turned their backs on him—his family, the few friends he'd trusted, the church into which he'd poured his life. They were the rats and he was the sinking ship.

Why had he given his life to a god who tormented him? Well, this was the end. From now on, he would live for himself. If Anne wouldn't stand by him, he would divorce her. If Robert didn't want to see him, he could go his own way. Collapsing on his back, David covered his face with his hands and wept.

Twenty minutes later, he dried his tears and washed his face. He had just lain back down when the door opened. "Come on Padgett, your lawyer wants to see you," the officer said as he kept one hand on the door, the other on his pepper gas container.

"You mean that kid?" David glared back at the officer. "What if I don't want to meet with him?"

"That's up to you," the officer said, closing the door.

"Wait, wait," David said, jumping up from the bunk and shoving his feet into his shoes. Swinging open the door, the officer grinned and shook his head. "Aren't you going to handcuff me?" David asked flippantly.

"You're just going down the hallway to the conference room. Whaddaya being so high and mighty for, Padgett? Most of these guys never see their lawyer until they go to court."

When they were halfway down the hall, he ordered David to "Stop!"

Through the window in the door, David saw the kid from the courtroom sitting at a steel table. David stepped into the room without acknowledging him and took a seat at the far end of the table.

"They give you a radio downstairs?" the officer asked the bright-eyed young attorney.

"Yes sir," he confirmed, holding up a box type radio.

"Okay. Just press that little orange button if he gets out of hand."

"This… this one?" the neophyte counselor asked, pointing to a recessed button on the top of the radio and stealing a nervous glimpse at David.

"Don't push it!" the officer shouted. "If you do, this place goes on lockdown and you'll have officers climbing all over you." Stepping out, the officer closed the door, locked it and was gone.

The kid scooted his chair a couple of feet closer to the door. David frowned at him. "You think I did everything they're saying."

"Uh… No." The paper he held rattled a little. "Let's get started."

David suddenly lurched forward, his hands shooting out across the table. The young lawyer scrambled backward, his chair scrapping against the concrete floor His face paled, his hands trembled, his finger was poised above the orange button.

"Great, that's just what I need, a lawyer who believes I'm guilty."

"Mr. er… Reverend Padgett, I'm here trying to help you."

"Am I your first client?"

The kid cleared his throat. "I assure you, Reverend, I am fully qualified to defend you and will do so to the best of my ability."

"When did you pass the bar, yesterday?"

139

Barlow looked a little miffed. "No, sir, not yesterday. The day before. And I did so on my first try. Some don't pass until their second or third."

"Wonderful," David grumbled as he stared past the young man. "Well, we have something in common. This is the first time I've been on trial for my life."

"I have some good news for you," Barlow said, handing a document to David.

"What's this?" David asked, scanning the sheet.

"A plea agreement. I persuaded the prosecutor to recommend a sentence of fifty years. You'll be eligible for parole in twenty-five."

"You want me to plead guilty to something I didn't do and spend the next twenty-five to fifty years of my life in prison?"

"If we go to trial the prosecutor is going to seek the death penalty."

David stared at Barlow until he blinked and looked away. "Have you even looked at the evidence?

"I'm sorry, as you know I was just assigned the case this morning."

"Get out!"

The kid looked at him wide-eyed. "Excuse me?"

"Press the talk button on your radio and tell them you want to leave."

"But we haven't discussed—"

"Either leave on your own or I'll fire you. How will that look on your record?"

"Okay, okay, Reverend." Flustered, Barlow pressed the orange button. "I'm ready to go now," he said to the radio as alarms blared and feet began pounding down the hall.

"You pushed the wrong button!" David shouted. His shaking hands reached for the radio. "Here, give it to me!"

Keys jangled in the lock. Five officers rushed in and pulled David from the chair, throwing him face down to the floor. He cried out as one of them jammed a knee into the small of his back. Another one yanked his arms behind him and roughly snapped on the cuffs.

# Chapter 21

Out of options, Anne picked up the phone in the living room. The sound of Russell's men tearing apart her kitchen unhinged her. There was a crash, then laughter. She flinched. Her desire to leave this place increased 100-fold. Trembling with nervous upset, she punched in the numbers. The phone rang six times. She was about to hang up when a sleepy voice answered.

"This is Lane Liston," he said hoarsely.

"Brother Liston, I'm sorry to call so early."

"That's perfectly all right, Mrs. Padgett. Normally I'm up long before this. One of our dearest couple's sons went to be with the Lord last night."

"Oh, I'm so sorry," Anne said, the dam almost bursting.

"I don't mean to trouble you. The good Lord knows you have enough of your own," Lane said. "How can I help you, Anne?"

Swallowing her tears, Anne quickly filled Liston in on Tibb Russell's actions. "Hang in there, Anne. Let me make a few calls. We have some farmers and retired men in our church," Lane said, his voice soft and gentle. "David is to be arraigned this morning, isn't he?"

"Yes, at nine."

"I'll pick up a truck and we'll have a crew at your house before noon."

Anne heard voices in the background. "Just a minute, Anne," Lane said. More muffled conversation. Anne's heart skipped a beat. If Liston's congregation objected, where could she go?

Many years ago, when David first entered the ministry, he asked Anne to accompany him as he preached at the Rescue Mission in Indianapolis. The smell of unwashed bodies almost overwhelmed her. Her heart went out to the hungry-looking children in soiled, ill-fitting clothes staring up at her with empty eyes. "Oh Lord, don't make me go there."

Lane came back on the line. "Anne, my wife was wondering if you have any special diet needs."

"Ah, no, no, thank you."

"Now you're welcome to eat with us or we can bring meals to the—"

"Any arrangement is fine. I'm so grateful to you and your church," Anne said. The dam sprang a leak.

"My wife is going to call the ladies of the church. They'll have the room in tiptop shape by this afternoon. And Anne, they know to keep this quiet. Well, as quiet as it can be."

"Are you sure you want the wife of an accused murderer staying at your church?" Anne asked reluctantly but feeling she had to.

Lane laughed long and hard. "Anne," he finally said, "I was thinking of your reputation, not mine. You forget I spent time in federal prison."

"Thank you, Lane. Thank you," Anne said, relief replacing her tears.

"Hang in there Anne. We'll be praying for you."

Anne hung up the phone and sat staring at it. Conviction sent an arrow through her heart. When Lane was arrested she had ridiculed the man of God and questioned his wife's wisdom for standing by him. She remembered making comments to her staff about the bunch of bumpkins who didn't know enough to fire the man. While in federal lock-up, Liston pastored his church from his prison cell. Now this same pastor, his wife and their church were standing by David and her.

She tried Robert's cell phone for the umpteenth time. She expected his voice mail to answer as it had throughout the night. When a strong male voice answered, it startled and distressed her.

"Hello?"

"Where's Robert?"

"He's indisposed. Can I take a message?"

"This is his mother, and I demand to speak to him," Anne said, edginess causing her voice to quiver. There was a hurried conversation behind a cupped hand, then, "Ma'am, this is Sergeant John Ralston with the Ottawa County, Missouri, Sheriff's Department."

"Oh no, has Robert been in an accident? Is he all right? Why can't I speak to him?" Anne thought her tears had ended. Yet more came as she waited to hear the fate of her son.

"Ma'am, I'm sorry but your son, Robert Kinkaid, was arrested this morning for robbery and murder," Ralston said.

"Kinkaid?" Anne bristled. She was thoroughly confused and more than a little irritated and she didn't try to hide it. "My son's name is Padgett, Robert Padgett," she said sharply.

"Would you describe your son for me, please?"

"He's five-nine, weighs about a hundred and ninety, he has dark brown hair and hazel eyes. He has a half circle scar on his left cheek. Let's see—"

"That's good enough, ma'am," Ralston interrupted. "Yes, that description fits the man we have in custody. He's suspected of killing the clerk at the Sleepy Time Motel at 2:30 this morning." Darkness swam before Anne's eyes. Still gripping the phone, she fell to the floor in a dead faint.

Robert woke up to find himself in a nightmare. He raised his head, wincing at the bump on his forehead. A disembodied, reverberating voice commanded, "Driver, get out of the car and keep your hands where I can see them." Robert was paralyzed with fear. All around him red and blue lights flashed. His fevered eyes saws 100 guns pointed at his head. He sat there in a dream state until the repeated shouts jolted his reflexes into action. The command came again, even more harshly. "Driver, this is your last warning! Throw out your weapon and exit the vehicle now!"

"I don't have a weapon," Robert cried, thrusting his arms through the open window. His mind screamed at him: They're going to kill you, shoot you down like a dog in the street.

"With your left hand, open the door," Sergeant Ralston shouted, training his handgun on Robert's head. One false move and it would be all over. They had hit the airways 20 minutes after arriving at the motel. Using the elderly man's description, special alerts were broadcast on every TV and radio station within a hundred-mile radius from 3 AM on. The farmer's call came at 6:55.

Within minutes, three sheriff's cars, two state police and even a couple of small town marshals were rolling. Shutting off their sirens a mile away, they converged on the suspect's vehicle from two directions. Ralston prayed each man would hold his position. His adrenaline surged as it flowed to his trigger finger. One false move and he could end up with a dead suspect and his department in hot water.

The car door swung open. "Stop!" Robert froze. "Keeping your hands up, step out of the vehicle." Ralston yelled. Throwing the bullhorn back into the patrol car, he gripped his pistol with both hands. Robert came out of the car. His body shook violently as he looked all around him, his eyes wild with fear. Ralston almost felt sorry for the man. "Lay on the ground face down," he called.

Robert dropped to the gravel road. The sharp, pointy stones assaulted his face; moisture from last night's rain penetrated his clothes. "Don't shoot, please don't shoot me," he cried, tears dripping into the small puddle under his nose. The smell of his own fear choked him. He could taste the coldness of death a hair's breath away as footsteps came at him.

The officer jerked his arms behind his back. Steel bands closed around his wrists. He felt hands yanking out his pants pockets. Someone grabbed his ankles and pulled off his shoes. He thought about the false driver's license he had printed from his computer. The only name he could think to use was Robert Kincaid, the character of his favorite book, *The Bridges of Madison County*. A dozen hands hauled him to his feet and slammed him against the hood of his car. A state trooper rifling through his wallet said, "Mr. Kincaid, you're in a world of hurt. Paul, read this slimeball his rights," he told another trooper standing nearby.

The ride to the Ottawa County Jail was to Robert deja vu of the scene less than 48 hours ago. Only now he was the one being hauled in, not his father. The line of police cars speeding down the interstate replicated those in Grafton. How quickly he had run from his father's trouble. The loneliness and despair he felt hollowed out his heart. He felt deserted, with not one person to care what happened to him. His life was in shambles.

"May, oh May, I am so, so sorry," Robert murmured, hanging his head. Tears splattered in small circles on his dark pants. "Why didn't I realize how wonderful our life was together?" At the jail, they pulled Robert out of the patrol car, hustled him inside, fingerprinted, photographed, relieved him of his clothing and tossed him an orange jumpsuit.

Sitting dazed on the steel bunk of holding cell number three, Robert rubbed his wrists as his mind traveled backward. Last month he was assistant pastor of one of the largest churches in the world. The governor of Indiana had welcomed him into his home. Last year he and his beautiful wife had dined at the White House. His father had spoken many times about stepping down from the leadership of Grace Tabernacle sometime in the next five years. "As soon as the mortgage on the church is paid off you can take over the church and broadcast ministry," he told Robert.

"What will you do, Dad?" Robert had asked perfunctorily, thinking the money would be great if nothing else.

Robert slipped off the bunk onto his knees and bowed his head. Unseen, two white beings descended through the ceiling. Their robes shone with a brilliant glow. Raising their jeweled swords, they stood guard over the kneeling man. Dark figures crawled over the walls of the jail, their fiery, darting eyes never leaving the guardian angels.

Throughout the years, Robert heard his father preach about trusting God. He himself had preached of reliance on the Lord. But the wages of sin never made their way to either of their pulpits. In seminary, Robert's favorite professor ridiculed the passages in the Bible that spoke of sin and laughed at those who cried out to God to save them.

A sharp rap on the metal door brought him rudely back to the moment. An elderly, balding man was looking through the small window in the middle of the door. Two more invisible, shining beings hovered over the old man. Hoisting himself to his feet, Robert approached the window.

"Hello, Robert. I'm Albert Frasier, the jail chaplain," he said with a kindly smile. "I know you're going through a rough time right now. Would you like me to pray with you?"

Robert looked into old man's gentle, peaceful face and tender eyes that spoke of godly love. Broken-hearted, tears flowed down Robert's cheeks. "Could you show me how to be saved?" he asked, his voice quavering.

Frasier was stunned. Was this not Robert Padgett, heir to the throne of Grace Tabernacle? Quickly recovering, he said, "Of course." Turning his head, he called, "John, would you open number three?" There was a whirr followed by a metallic click. Robert stepped back as the heavy steel door slid open.

"Thank you," Frasier called to the officer. Stepping through the opening, he held out his hand. As Robert took it, the door slid closed. The two shining beings watching over the preacher remained outside the cell, their swords drawn, their eyes moving in all directions. Sitting on the bunk next to Robert, the preacher opened a well-worn Bible.

For the next few minutes, he read verses from the books of Romans, First Corinthians and Ephesians. Though Robert had heard Bible readings all his life, the scriptures seemed new and fresh to him. Finally coming back to Romans, the old preacher read one more verse. "Whosoever shall call upon the name of the Lord shall be saved. That means you, son," Frasier said, laying his hand on Robert's shoulder. "Would you like to be saved right now?"

Lifting his tear-stained face, Robert said, "Yes sir, I sure would." The dark figures hissed and attempted to come forward, but fear of the angels' swords kept them back.

"That's wonderful, Robert," Frasier said, smiling brightly. "Now, you can repeat a prayer after me or pray on your own, whichever is better for you."

Bowing his head, Robert's stumbling words entreated. "Lord, you know what a mess I've made of my life." He paused, his voice choked with tears. He cleared his throat quietly. "I... I've been a hypocrite for years, pretending to be a Christian. Now I want the real thing. Please come into my heart and forgive my sins and be my Savior. Amen."

A brilliant smile spread across Robert's face as he wiped the tears from his cheeks. "Now, son," Frasier said, placing his arm across the younger man's shoulders, "you're a new creation in Jesus Christ."

At that moment, the cell door opened and an officer stood frowning just outside. "Okay, Padgett, come with me.

Chapter 22

Anne awoke with a start. Something wet was touching her face. Warily, she opened her eyes to see a petite woman kneeling beside her holding a damp facecloth. "Lane and I were really concerned when we found you on the floor."

It all came rushing back. Her husband, her son, both were in jail, both accused of murder. She started to cry, shaking with big, heaving sobs. Betty Liston held the woman to her breast, comforting her as she would a small child. Lane appeared in the kitchen doorway, questioning his wife with his eyes.

Over Anne's head, Betty mouthed the word "Pray." Lane nodded and slipped quietly away. The sound of the men moving furniture came to a halt as Pastor Liston, the men from Pine Bluff Baptist and Chief Donald Price knelt in prayer. After several minutes, Betty held Anne slightly away from her and said tenderly, "Anne, you know God loves you."

Trembling, Anne replied, "Yes."

"And you know all things work together for good to them who love God and are called according to his purpose. And God has definitely called David and you into the ministry."

"But I don't love God. I've been so wicked and sinful. I spoke to three thousand women in Atlanta and instead of praying for their souls, I..." Anne drew a shuddering breath. "I got drunk. And I only agreed to speak there so I could buy a new car."

"Anne, God's love doesn't depend on our being good. If it did, we would all be on our way to hell." Anne's sobs subsided. She laid her head on Betty's shoulder. Betty could feel dampness from Anne's tears soaking through her blouse. The tinge of expensive perfume touched her nose. Betty bought her perfume at Walmart, but she recognized the fragrance as Chanel No. 5. Yet she felt no resentment. This was God's child she held in her arms. "Anne, look at me,"

Betty said. Anne raised her head, her eyes swimming. "Do you love your son?"

"Yes, of course I do."

"What if he did something really, really bad? Would you still love him?" Betty asked, her eyes radiating compassion.

"Certainly. I would love him because he's my son," Anne said, wondering if Betty knew Robert was in jail in Missouri.

"Your love for Robert is because of your relationship to him, not his behavior." Anne nodded. "In the same way, God loves us because we are his children through Jesus Christ."

Anne's mind drifted back to the ministry she and David once had at the old Steuben County Jail. How many times had she made statements similar to that to the women behind bars?

Rising slightly, Anne knelt on the floor beside Betty. Betty took her hand. Anne began to pray aloud, a prayer of repentance and rededication to the Lord. When she finished, the two women continued to kneel together with their heads bowed. Neither of them heard the front door open.

"Well, isn't this sweet?" Tibb Russell sneered as he stood over them. "The tax cheat's and the murderer's wives praying together. I hope you're praying for a place to live, because I want you out of here in exactly...," he looked at his watch, "three hours and twenty minutes."

Donald Price, Lane Liston and two husky men in bib overalls came in from the kitchen. "I'm glad to see the police are here," Russell said, looking at Don. "Chief, if they're still here at one minute after four I want you to arrest them for trespassing."

"I should arrest you," Don said, resting his hands on his hips.

"On what charge?" Russell blustered. Something passed over his eyes and quickly vanished.

"Indecent exposure," Don said. "Exposing yourself as the hypocrite you really are."

"One minute after four, Chief, or I'll have your badge."

"You don't own my badge," Don said, tapping the star-shaped medal on his chest. "Or me."

150

"You'd be surprised what I own," Tibb Russell snapped. Turning on his heel, he stormed out, slamming the door behind him.

"Oh dear, I'm sorry," Anne said as she got to her feet. "I'm afraid I've caused trouble for all of you."

"Nonsense," Lane said. "There's nothing I enjoy more than fighting Satan's minions."

The group followed Don into the kitchen. Stepping to the window over the sink, Don watched Russell march across the lawn to his car. "Anne, you didn't start this," the police chief said. "I've suspected Russell of illegal activity for quite some time. I just haven't been able to prove it."

"What kind of activity?" Lane asked.

"There was a rumor two years ago that the state attorney general was getting ready to indict Russell for fraud. The insurance commissioner was closing in on him for selling worthless policies. Then it just all blew over."

"I heard he's almost broke. Any truth to that?" Lane prodded.

"I don't know," Don said, "could be. The hurricane in the Gulf almost wiped out him out."

Every head turned to look incredulously at Anne when she said, "He wanted me to marry him. He said if I did I could keep the house." The men shook their heads. Betty laid a comforting hand on Anne's arm.

"Well, folks, I hate to say it but we have to keep going with the move," Don said. "He'll have us arrested if we're here past four."

"Can he do that?" one of the farmers asked.

"Yeah, I'm afraid he can," Don said, walking toward the stairs.

"Then we better get cracking," the other farmer said.

At 3:50, Russell returned. Standing like a sentry on the grass at the edge of the driveway, he watched the final items being loaded into the truck. Leaving the others to finish up, Don went outside to speak to him. Standing at the kitchen window, Anne couldn't hear what was being said. However,

Russell's red face and angry gestures made it clear he didn't like it. A minute later Tibb shoved open the back gate and stormed off. Don returned with a sad smile on his face.

With two minutes to go, the last box was slid into the back of the truck. Leaving all the furniture and taking nothing from the kitchen, Ann had packed only her and David's personal items.

"Let's pray," Lane said, kneeling on the grass and holding out his hands. The others followed suit, forming a circle. "Lord, we thank you for the ministry you have given our brother and sister at Grace Tabernacle. We leave here not knowing what the future holds. We trust you to do as you said, work all things for our good. Help us to be obedient. We ask this in Jesus' name, amen."

Lane climbed in behind the wheel of the U-Haul. One of the farmers rode shotgun and the other followed in his pickup. Anne knew there was something she had to do. She spoke to Betty as she got into her 10-year-old Chevy. "Betty, would you follow me?"

"Of course," Betty said.

As the caravan pulled away from the mansion, Anne watched that part of her life fall away. In the rear view mirror, Grace Tabernacle became smaller and smaller. Sad but relieved, Anne sighed and pulled the Roadster to the front of the caravan. Just one more thing to do and she would be free. At Allan Motors, she drove into the lot as the others stopped along the curb.

"Well, Mrs. Padgett, what can I do for you?" Allan asked as Anne entered his office. "Shall we upgrade you to the top of the line?" He leaned back in his chair, a strained smile on his ruddy face. A garishly-colored oil painting of the automotive bigwig hung above his head. The facial expression reminded Anne of a badger ready to strike. She swallowed, took a deep breath, and plunged ahead.

"Mr. Allan, I am returning the Mercedes Roadster I purchased two months ago," Anne declared with forced assertiveness. Allan's oily smile was quickly replaced by a hard frown that seemed more natural for him.

"And what, pray tell, am I supposed to do with a murderer's wife's used car?" he asked, biting off each word. He pursed his mouth as if sucking on something sour.

"My husband is accused, not convicted, Mr. Allan," Anne said, her words firm and steady. "And even if the court finds him guilty, I never will. I will believe in David's innocence until my dying day."

"Be that as it may," Allan said, tossing his pen on the desk, "I don't want that car on my lot. It will attract lookie-loos and nosy reporters."

From the spot just outside the office door where he'd been listening, Lane stepped in. "Mr. Allan, this automobile has only a few thousand miles on it. Mrs. Padgett has paid two installments plus a large down payment. So you've already gotten more than you would if it were used," Lane said, his voice soft and persuasive.

"My accounts are frozen, Mr. Allan, even the royalties from my husband's books. I have no way to pay you," Anne said. Allan's brow furrowed into a deep scowl.

"You know, the cars on your lot really shine," Lane said, not quite as friendly this time. "You suppose I could talk to the men who washed them and ask how they do such a good job?"

Allan looked threateningly at him. "My employees can't be disturbed."

"I see. Well, would they even understand me if I were to speak to them?" Lane asked, raising his eyebrows knowingly.

"I want both of you off these premises at once!" Allan yelled as he jumped to his feet and waved angrily toward the door.

"Sure, we're leaving, but before we do, could I borrow your phone book?" Lane asked, smiling. "I want to look up the number for ICE."

Allan paled. "Now, now, let's be reasonable. I'm sure we can work something out," he said, rubbing his hands together.

"I believe returning Mrs. Padgett's down payment and the two installments would be reasonable," Lane said, knowing nothing of the demand made by Rose Turner of Women's Rejoice.

"Fine," Allan grumbled, pulling a checkbook from the middle desk drawer.

"I do believe Mrs. Padgett would prefer cash," Lane said, more as a demand than a suggestion.

"Yes, I think that would be best," Anne agreed. She and Lane returned Allan's steely gaze. He held his scowl for a moment, then his face went flat. With no further words, he stepped behind his desk and pulled at the corner of the paint-by-numbers portrait. The painting swung out, revealing a safe. Blocking their view, Allan spun the dial and opened the door. Removing a large stack of bills, he closed everything up and sat down at the desk with a heavy sigh. He fished a sheet of paper from a drawer, wrote a few lines and he pushed it over to Anne.

"This releases me and you from any further contractual obligation," he said quietly as he counted out the money. Then more forcefully, "However, if that automobile is damaged in any way, it gives me the right to assess repair costs."

Anne read the few lines and signed. She and Lane smiled at each other as Allan stepped out to make a copy. Taking the original from his hand, she said, "Thank you," picked up the cash and headed out the door.

"Please, if you require the services of a dealership in the future, go somewhere else," Allan called after them, his voice resuming its harshness.

Leaving Grafton in Betty's car, a surge of freedom gladdened Anne's heart.

## Chapter 23

Flanked by the old chaplain and an cfficer, Robert walked out of the cell to the book-in area of the jail. The four celestial beings glided alongside with their swords at the ready. The officer stopped. Robert felt a calmness he had never known before. Many times he had preached on the peace which passes all understanding. Although a part of him knew it to be true, he never experienced it until today.

Frasier sensed that something astonishing was happening. It was against jail policy to remove a prisoner from a cell unrestrained. The officer led the two men to the door of a small room and opened it. The officer behind the desk stepped to the counter and laid a piece of paper in front of Robert.

"Sign here," he said, indicating an "X" under several bulleted lines of type.

"What is this?" Robert asked, looking from the sheet to the officer.

"It's a receipt stating you have received your property and nothing was damaged," the officer said. "If upon inspecting it you find that some item is damaged, you will be required to complete another form."

"I don't understand," Robert said, locking at the chaplain.

"You're being released, Reverend Padgett. We caught the perpetrator three hours ago. He was good enough to confess to the robberies and the murder," the first officer said. Robert heaved a huge sigh as he took the pen held out by the beaming Frasier and signed.

The second officer handed him a bag containing his clothes and personal items. "The DA has decided not to prosecute you for your little deception."

"Deception?" Frasier queried.

"It seems the good reverend had a license identifying him as one of the main characters in *The Bridges of Madison*

155

*County*," the first officer explained with a chuckle. "Said license has been destroyed."

"I apologize for that," Robert said. "I didn't want anyone to know my name is Padgett."

"I can understand that," the officer allowed. "The name Padgett is not exactly highly-favored right now. Your car is in the impound lot. I'll give them a call."

"I'll show him where it is. Thanks, gentlemen," Frasier said as the second officer led Robert through a side door to change his clothes.

As they waited for Robert's car to be brought around, Frasier handed him his card. "Son, if you forget everything else, remember God loves you. The trials you've faced and will in the future will only serve to make you stronger."

Tears streamed down Robert's face as he grabbed the old man and hugged him. "God bless you, Chaplain. All these years I didn't even realize I wasn't saved. Whatever happens now, the Lord and I will handle it together."

"Call me anytime you need someone to talk to," the chaplain said, laying his hand on Robert's shoulder. "We have a service here tonight. If it's all right with you, I'll share your testimony with the prisoners."

"Yes, please tell them. Tell the whole world!" Robert exclaimed, smiling widely through his tears. He looked into the preacher's transparent blue eyes clear to his soul. For the first time in his life, he was basking in the pure light of agape love.

Smiling, the old preacher said, "Let's have a word of prayer before you go." The old gospel warrior and the new child of God bowed their heads. "Lord, we praise you and thank you for saving Robert. I pray you will bless him and help him to live for you. May many lives be touched by his testimony. In Jesus' name, amen."

Breathing the sweet air of God's mercy, Robert headed east on the interstate. At the Ottawa County line, he pulled into the emergency lane. As semis and other vehicles whizzed past, Robert bowed his head. "Father, thank you for saving me. Help me to live a life pleasing to you." A sob caught in his throat. "Please tell May I love her and that I am so, so sorry for betraying her." He remained there for a few more minutes, then, glancing quickly into his side-view mirror, pulled out.

Joe Madison was running late. He pressed harder on the accelerator. The speedometer climbed to 65, then 70 and leveled off at 75. Ten years and hundreds of thousands of miles driving for Federal Express bolstered Joe's confidence. He had never had an accident, never even came close. Snow, sleet, rain or sunny days, it made no difference. You could count on Joe to get your widget through.

He spotted the green, late model Cadillac sitting at the side of the road a half-mile ahead. Glancing into his side-view mirror, Joe saw a mid-sized motor home in the left lane racing along at the midway point of his tandem trailers. The Cadillac loomed closer and very soon he'd be squeezed between the two. He didn't like having to pass so close to disabled vehicles.

Joe was excited. Tonight was his son's fifth birthday party. In Kansas City, he had stopped at a mall and bought a remote control ATV for Mikey. He couldn't wait to see the look on the boy's face when he opened his present. The box sat on the seat beside Joe. Laying his hand on the package, he smiled and brought the semi up to a smooth 77. The engine hummed.

Distracted, Joe didn't see the Cadillac begin to move; in truth he never saw it budge until it was halfway into his lane. He slammed on the brakes and hit the air horn. The big rig's screeching tires, blaring horn and irrepressible momentum pierced Joe's heart with terror. "Oh, dear Lord, help me!" he screamed as he stood on the brakes, his hips two inches above the seat. Shaking wildly, the rear trailer swung sideways into the left lane.

Lulled by the monotony of the road, the motor home's gray-haired driver snapped to his senses. Looking in his rearview mirror, he saw the side of the second trailer 10 feet from the back of his vehicle. There was a piercing shriek of tearing metal as it struck the motor home's rear. Sitting beside him, his wife screamed. The semi's tractor was edging into their lane. The elderly man slammed the gas pedal to the floorboard. The motor home was maxed out. Instantly he made the deadly decision to pull the left front wheel onto the median.

For a few precious seconds he thought he could hold it. Then the motor home's left front tire twisted. Flipping end over end, the hulking vehicle smashed down on its top and skidded into the west bound lane. A teenager in an old Mustang ended the couple's lives. Miraculously surviving, the young man would be haunted for the rest of his life by the horror in the elderly couple's faces seconds before the grill of his car smashed through their windshield and snuffed out their lives.

With the motor home out of his path, Joe tried to wrestle the semi into the left lane. The heavily-loaded truck would have none of it. Twenty feet from the Cadillac's driver's door, Joe saw the man look up. For the briefest second they looked into each other's eyes. Two strangers were about to die simultaneously. The bumper of the Fed Ex behemoth careened into the driver's door of the Cadillac. The green car flew through the air like a crumpled toy being tossed away by a child tired of playing with it.

The car smashed down tail first 150 feet away. The impact ruptured the gas tank; fuel poured onto the roadway. The car flipped onto its side. Sparks flew as it skidded on the asphalt. Still conscious, Robert felt a peacefulness envelop him.

The tractor cab came to rest on its side. The trailers sprawled across the traffic lanes, bringing everything behind them to a screeching halt. Interstate 70 would be shut down for the next four hours as highway crews cleared the carnage. Hanging by his seat belt, Joe never made it home for his son's fifth birthday, or his sixth, or his seventh.

The toy ATV had tumbled to the floor of the cab and was undamaged. A state trooper delivered it to Joe's widow three days after the accident. Mikey never played with it, never even opened the box. He placed it on a shelf in his room as a memorial to the father he would barely remember.

With a whoosh, fire erupted in the gas pool 20 feet behind the Cadillac. It raced up the oily stream and enveloped the vehicle. Robert felt no pain, only a sense of joy, a thrill like none he'd ever known. He looked down at his legs trapped under the steering wheel. They were on fire. The dashboard and steering wheel melted before his eyes. The fire engulfing him grew more intense until it gave off a brilliant, beautiful light. The light dissolved into a magnificent landscape. Children played under huge trees, their laughter ringing across lush, grassy meadows. A marvelous shining radiance just ahead shimmered in the light that seemed to encompass him.

Endless fields of flowers filled his vision. Roses of every variety and hue intermingled all the way to the horizon with other rainbow-colored blooms Robert had never seen. A glorious temple seemed to grow out of the terrain and rise up into the brilliant blue sky. The odors of gasoline, burning plastic and flesh and death were overtaken by a sweet, honey like aroma. Somewhere a choir sang. The ethereal music and crystal clear words caressed Robert's ears.

*Worthy is the lamb that was slain,*
*worthy is the lamb that was slain.*
*To receive glory and honor,*
*to receive glory and honor,*
*to receive glory and honor,*
*worthy is the lamb that was slain.*

The angelic chorus rose to a thrilling crescendo before the song faded away, then began again. Robert found himself singing with the choir. Amazingly, he knew the words and melody.

A lovely small child with bouncing blonde curls ran up to Robert and hugged him around his legs. He reached down and smoothed her hair. "What a beautiful child," he said. His voice sounded strange to him. There was a musical quality to it that he didn't recognize. "Do you live around here, sweetheart?"

The child looked up at him with the clearest blue eyes. They seemed to be transparent. "This is my home now," she said with a dazzling smile. Turning in a circle with a sweep of her arm, she indicated the entire panorama. Robert picked her up. She was light as a feather. She rested comfortably in his arms as if she were used to being there.

Strolling with her to the grove where the children played, Robert asked, "What's your name, little one?"

"My mommy named me before I was born," she said, a brilliant smile lighting her face. The illumination seemed to come from within. "Precious."

"And your last name, Precious?" Robert asked, knowing the answer but feeling compelled to ask.

"Ridgeway," the little girl answered, hugging Robert tightly around the neck. Then, leaning back in his arms, she looked him in the face. The smile never left her lips. "Are you my daddy?"

"Yes, Precious. Yes, I am," Robert said, hugging the child tightly. His tears came in big drops.

"Don't cry, Daddy," the little girl said. Wriggling out of his arms, she smiled up at him and took him by the hand. "We'll go see Jesus. He'll wipe the tears from your eyes. You will never cry again. When Mommy first came here, Jesus wiped away her tears. Now she's happy all the time." She tugged him in the direction of the temple, leading him down a path paved with gold.

As they rounded a bend, two figures in shining white garments came toward them. Letting go of Robert's hand, Precious ran to the woman on the left. "Mommy! Mommy! Daddy's here!" Grasping Ellen's hand, the child tugged her forward.

"Yes, dear, isn't that wonderful?" Ellen said, smiling first at Precious, then at the man standing before her.

Robert hung his head. "I'm sorry, Ellen. I'm so sorry."

"Robert, how could I be angry with you?" Ellen asked. "Because of what happened on earth, I'll have my sweet little daughter with me for eternity."

The second figure stepped forward. "May, oh my darling, beautiful May," Robert cried, tears streaming down his face. "How I've missed you." Husband and wife fell into each other's arms.

"Everything is all right now," May said, her smile as glorious as a sunrise. An overwhelming joy flowed through Robert's being. "Come, let us go into the presence of our Lord," May said. Together, husband and wife, mother and daughter walked hand-in-hand down the golden path to the temple of the Living God.

# Chapter 24

Back in his cell, David stared at himself in the stainless steel mirror bolted to the wall. The metal distorted his image, giving him a wavy appearance; still he could see the dark bruises on his cheek. "At least they complete the look," he muttered as he turned his face to study his black eye and blood-crusted nose. He rubbed his arms. They felt almost as though they'd been torn from their sockets.

There was a rattling of keys in the cell door. It swung open. A large man in a blue uniform stood in the opening. With the light behind him, David couldn't see his face.

"Pastor, are you all right?" Don Price asked, concern in his face and voice.

"Oh, sure, Don, I'm just dandy," David said, his face an angry mask. "I'm being tried for murder, correction, three murders. I've been convicted by the media. Even my own lawyer thinks I'm guilty. I've been used as a human punching bag by inmates and officers. Yeah, Don, I'm doing just great."

"I know it's been rough, but hang in there," Don said. "I may have some good news for you."

"My sad excuse for a lawyer had good news for me, too," David scoffed. "He got me a plea agreement for fifty years."

"I know, I just spoke to him," Don said. "David, the sheriff wants you out of here. You're too—"

"That makes two of us," David interjected.

Don smiled slightly. "You're too high-profile to keep in the jail. They're sending you to a holding facility at the state prison in Carlisle." Don looked down at his shoes.

"You're taking me to prison?" David said, raising his voice. "I haven't even been convicted."

"You'll be safer there," Price said, his voice barely above a whisper.

"What's going on, Don? Tell me," David said, his heart racing.

"Sit down," Don said, lowering himself down to the steel bunk and patting the thin mattress. Even in the hot cell, a chill came over David. Sitting down next to Don, he looked at his friend.

"David, I believe your life is in danger." Don raised his hand to stop David from speaking. "Someone is manipulating the evidence on Ellen Ridgeway's suicide to make it look like she was murdered."

Fear stirred in David's heart. "What about Linda Darby?"

"The evidence there is really strong. The ring, the fingerprints, worst of all the call she made to nine-one-one," Don said, running his hands along his thighs. "We have to attack each incident separately."

"Don, do you think I'm guilty?" David asked, his eyes probing his friend's.

"David... Pastor, we've been friends for a long time. Everything I know points to your innocence. You've dedicated your life to the Lord. No! I don't believe you murdered anyone."

David exhaled without realizing he'd been holding his breath. "Thank you," he said, smiling for the first time since the ordeal began.

"I need you to be patient," Price cautioned. "It may take some time to prove your innocence."

"Who do you suspect?"

"For your own safety, I'd rather not say."

"When am I leaving?" David thought about Anne and Robert. "Would it be possible to see my wife and son before I do?"

"I'll try to arrange a visit," Price said. "But the sheriff is keeping this very hush-hush. I may not be able to. Pastor, why don't you lead us in prayer?"

The two men bowed their heads. David tried to speak. His voice choked. He tried again. Finally he said, "Go ahead, Don."

Price hesitated. His pastor's spiritual condition was devastating. Haltingly, Don prayed for David's protection and spiritual renewal and for wisdom for himself to find the killer.

After Don left, David lay on his bunk. His mind raced. Who would do this to him? Why would anyone want to destroy him? One thought kept coming to him: his son. He tried to push it out of his mind. But the anger, the resentment, the infidelity— maybe Robert wasn't cut out for a life of service. Yet how many times had he preached to young marrieds about resolving anger before it became a festering sore?

Suddenly, David sat straight up and stared wide-eyed at the concrete wall. He couldn't remember a time when Robert received Christ as his savior. As the church grew, David became busy almost to the point of distraction. He barely saw his family from the time Robert was seven until he was 15. When he turned 17, David introduced him to the dark room. The first night the advisors stayed away. Likewise the next. On the third, Robert's boredom and disinterest were palpable.

"Just a few more minutes, son," David said, willing the ghostly counselors to appear. Five minutes later, a gauzy white apparition filtered through the wall. Robert's eyes were as big as saucers. When the figure materialized into a long-dead Abraham Lincoln, Robert ran screaming for the door and refused to have any part in it ever again.

David continued to meet with the spirits every night, sometimes for just a few minutes, sometimes for hours. When he asked their advice about Robert, all but the atheist Ingersoll advised him to be patient and wait for his son to come around. Ingersoll, on the other hand, ridiculed David and his beliefs.

From the first time Ingersoll had come into his presence, David wanted to be rid of the scornful old atheist. He asked Tibb Russell's advice on how to do it. Russell seemed perturbed. He argued that Ingersoll would make a great sounding board. "You're trying to reach the ones who don't go to church, aren't you?" Russell asked with a thin, cynical smile. David detected annoyance in Tibb's demeanor, as if he hadn't expected his practice of meeting with dead advisors to work for David and was jealous that it had.

"Yes," David said. "But this man was an enemy of God and every Christian believer."

"Exactly! Who better to endeavor to bring over to your side? Why, you might even persuade him to become a Christian."

"He's dead. The time of his decision is past," David answered, amazed at how little Russell knew about the Bible.

David was shaken out of his reverie by a voice at the door. "Let's go, Padgett." The officer opened the cuff port. "Detectives want to have a little talk with you."

After riding the elevator to the lower level, the officer guided him to a stark room with a table and three chairs. The officer pulled one out and motioned David to sit. Then he stood arms akimbo at the door. Across the room, a mirrored window reflected David's dishevelment.

In a few minutes, two men came through the door. "Hello, Doctor Padgett," one of them said, holding out his hand. Freed of his handcuffs, David shook it. "I'm Detective Spiegel, this is Detective Root." Root ignored David's outstretched hand.

Dropping his hand to his side, David asked warily, "Shouldn't my lawyer be present?"

Root and Spiegel laughed. "That kid?" Spiegel snorted. "My ten-year-old knows more about the law than he does."

"Besides, this was his idea," Root said, looking at his partner.

"Sure," Spiegel lied. "He said he couldn't be here, but to just go ahead, he trusts us."

"We want to know why you murdered that poor old woman," Root said. Still standing, he leaned across the table with his huge hands flat on its surface and glared at David.

Fear raced up David's spine. His heart pounded. "I didn't kill anyone," he said weakly. "I want to speak to my lawyer."

165

Root slammed down his fist on the metal table, making it bounce. The officer at the door jumped and reached for his pepper spray. Both detectives looked menacingly at David.

"Aren't you supposed to be a man of God? How can you live with yourself?" Spiegel tsk-tsked and shook his head.

"I'll tell you how," Root growled, his face inches from David's. "He's not human. You stinking hypocrite, I oughta just shoot you." The officer looked alarmed.

"Calm down, Root," Spiegel said, laying a restraining hand on his partner's arm.

Pulling his arm away, Root yelled, "Oh, you mean you think it's okay what he did?" He let loose a barrage of profanities. In 20 years of ministering to the public, David had not heard words so vulgar. The detective's face flamed; a vein pulsed in his neck.

"No, of course not." Spiegel's voice cracked. "No one could, seeing what he did to that poor old lady."

While Root stood glowering at Robert with his arms across his chest, Spiegel got up and walked to the door. The deputy opened it. A minute later, he came back with a manila envelope from which he spilled several large photos onto the table. Spreading them out before David, he said, "Here, have a look at your handiwork."

The detectives hurried out, pausing at the door only long enough for one of them to tell the deputy, "If he touches those pictures, break his arms."

Glaring at David, the deputy fingered the baton on his belt. As if by a magnet, David's eyes were drawn to the horror spread before him. Linda Darby lay in a pool of blood, a large butcher knife buried in her chest. Two of the pictures showed Ellen Ridgeway lying lifeless on her bed. He remembered standing over her and thinking she looked like a small child. Tears moistened his eyes.

On the other side of the mirror, Root slapped Spiegel on the back and chuckled. "A little melodramatic maybe, but a stellar performance nevertheless."

166

They watched as the preacher turned sideways in his chair to avert his eyes from the horrific images of gore and death.

"Hey, you sure the chief's gone for the day?" Spiegel asked his partner, glancing around nervously.

"Yeah, don't worry. The old man won't be back."

"Better not be. If he finds us interrogating Padgett without his lawyer, the least he'll do is suspend us."

"Or fire us," Root said, looking around the deserted squad room.

"Hey, here's an idea," Spiegel said, pulling his cell phone from his jacket pocket. "When you did that imitation of the kid you sounded just like him. I'll tell Padgett his lawyer wants to talk to him."

"Oh, man." Root grinned wickedly. "You think he'd fall for that?"

"Turn on the fan and tell him you're on the road. That thing sounds like a truck goin' uphill."

"Charlie, you're a genius," Root chuckled.

Back in the interrogation room, Spiegel handed his cell phone to David. "Your lawyer wants to have a word with you." Taking the phone, David held it to his ear.

"Reverend Padgett? This is Barlow. I hope you can hear me, the traffic is really loud," Root said, leaning closer to the fan.

The words were muffled and the voice didn't sound like Barlow's. "Go on," David said.

"Reverend, I've spoken to detectives Root and Spiegel. You can trust them. They're just trying to get to the truth," Root said into the phone, his face inches from the whirring fan. "Just tell them what you did and they'll help you. It'll be easier if you confess."

"I told you, you're fired!" David shouted. "Don't ever contact me again!" He threw the phone on the table. It skittered across the metal surface, scattering the photographs, then crashed to the concrete floor and broke apart. Spiegel leaped, trying in vain to catch the flying instrument. Gathering up the pieces, he shouted, "You piece of garbage! You're going to prison, and I'm gonna make sure you wind up in hell, just like your son."

The door flew open, almost smacking the deputy. Root barged in and ran at David, cocking back his arm. He punched David full force in the face. The blow rocked David's head so hard his chair keeled over backward. His head smacked the floor. Blackness floated before his eyes.

Root knelt over David. "Oh yeah, did we forget? Your wife wanted us to tell you your kid bought the farm in a car wreck this afternoon," he snarled into David's bloodless face. "She was bawling her brains out, just like the families of those women you killed."

# Chapter 25

Albert Frasier looked at the report, his eyes scanning the sheet. Three times he picked up the phone and started punching in the numbers. Three times he hit the end button. "It's not going to get easier," he said out loud. There was no one to hear. He sat alone in his broom-closet of an office. His scarred desk was bare except for a small stack of Bibles and this single sheet of paper.

This was the part of the job he hated. He could work all day counseling inmates, praying with them and their families and preaching the word of God. When it came to death notices... He shook his head to keep back the tears. Well, this one would be better than most. At least Robert Padgett was saved. A thrill came to his heart remembering the light in the redeemed young man's eyes. The chaplain didn't have many years left on this earth. As many souls as he could lead to the Savior would be his legacy.

Sitting on the bed in the prophet's chamber at Pine Bluff Baptist Church, Anne glanced at the clock. Six PM. Forty-eight hours ago her husband was pastor of one of the most famous mega churches in the world. Her son was co-pastor and she was on her way to realizing the career of her dreams. Now David and Robert sat in jail and she in this tiny room among furnishings that a week ago, if had been up to her, she would have donated to Goodwill.

The three of them had stopped being a family and become an organization having financial gain as its goal and pleasure as its pursuit. Yet now material things scarcely mattered. Despite everything going on, she felt a peace and contentment she hadn't experienced in years. Her past was buried, the future unknown.

Anne's father pastored small country churches throughout his adult life. On the day he died of a heart attack, he had taught Sunday school and preached the morning service. After lunch, he went upstairs for a nap. Two hours later, Anne's mother went to wake him. She found him on his knees at the bedside, his Bible open before him. His prayers for his people were on his lips when he died. Thinking of that now, Anne winced over the sad fact that she would not know most of the members of Grace Tabernacle if she met them on the street.

Her cell phone rang. Her heart leaped into her throat when she saw Ottawa County Jail on the screen. She hadn't known how to broach the subject of Robert's arrest with Lane and Betty. How do you explain that your son has indeed followed in his father's footsteps, yet hardly in the way you expected? Flipping open the phone, she held it between her thumb and forefinger as if it were the head of a snake. "Hello?"

Clearing his throat, the preacher said, "Hello, Mrs. Padgett? This is Albert Frasier. I'm the chaplain of the Ottawa County jail."

"Is my son all right?" Anne asked, rising to her feet. When Frasier hesitated, her heart began to race.

"I'm sorry," he finally said.

"Sorry about what? Is he hurt? How badly? What hospital is he in?" Anne cried as tears spilled down her cheeks.

"First let me tell you that Robert received Christ as his savior this morning."

Confused, Anne said, "Robert saved? But I thought he already was."

"Yes, yes, that is what your son believed. However, God showed him otherwise."

"Where is he?"

"This afternoon he was released from jail. The police found the real murderer and Robert was exonerated." Taking a deep breath, Frasier went on. "From there, we're not sure what happened. Mrs. Padgett, I'm sorry. Your son, Robert, was killed in an accident on I-70 today."

Collapsing to her knees, Anne screamed. Her heart cried out for the son she had carried in her womb. Still clutching the phone, she wailed, "Why? Oh why, God? Why now?"

170

The old preacher said, "I wish I could tell you why, Mrs. Padgett. One thing I can assure you of is that Robert is in heaven, more alive than ever before."

"Thank you, Reverend," Anne sobbed, meaning it.

After praying with her and making sure she had his office, cell and home numbers, Frasier said goodbye. Bowing his head, he prayed for Robert's grieving family. "And, Lord bring your servant David Padgett out of jail. Make him a greater leader than he ever was before. May many souls come into your kingdom because of him." Wearily, Chaplain Frasier went home to the wife who loved him.

Coming up the hallway toward the prophet's chamber, Betty heard loud sobbing. Reluctant to intrude yet wanting to comfort Anne, she knocked softly. Rising from her knees and wiping her face with the back of her hands, Anne said weakly, "Come in."

"Is there anything I can do, Anne?" Betty asked as she studied the woman's broken face.

"Oh Betty," Anne cried, falling into her friend's arms, "Robert was killed in a car accident." Feeling as if she was comforting Job's wife, Betty hugged Anne until her sobs quieted down. Not wanting to leave her alone, Betty led her to her husband's office. There Lane and Betty prayed with and for Anne Padgett.

"David needs to know," Anne said quietly, dabbing at her eyes with a tissue. "Before he hears it from the media."

"I'll take care of it, Anne. You try and get some rest," Lane said as he picked up the phone. "Betty, can you stay with Anne for a while?"

"Of course, hon."

Back in the prophet's chamber, Anne stretched out on the bed and covered her eyes with her forearm. "I know I should thank the Lord for Robert's life," she said, thinking of the time he fell out of the treehouse. "It just seems like our time on this earth is so short."

Sitting beside Anne, Betty patted her hand and said, "No matter how long we live, there's never enough time."

Praying for strength, Lane punched in the number for the Steuben County Sheriff's office. Passing by the book-in desk, Root picked up the phone. "Steuben County Jail."

"Yes sir, this is Lane Liston. I'm pastor of Pine Bluff Baptist and a friend of the Padgett family."

"Yeah?" Root said in a low growl, tempted to hang up.

"Is there a chaplain I can speak to?"

"He's gone for the day. Why do you want to talk to the chaplain?" Root brashly inquired.

"David Padgett's son, Robert Padgett, was killed today in an accident on the interstate in Ottawa County," Lane said, his voice breaking.

"Oh no!" Root exclaimed in mock horror. "That's terrible." He hoped his grin didn't come through in his voice. "It's hard enough being in jail without a loved one dying."

"Are you a Christian, sir?"

"Yes, yes." Lane detected a hint of facetiousness in Root's tone, but said nothing as the detective rattled on. "I attend Grace Tabernacle whenever I can. You know, crime doesn't take Sundays off."

"Perhaps I should come in and speak with Reverend Padgett," Lane suggested.

Root bristled. "That won't be necessary, Reverend. I'll speak to Dr. Padgett." He stifled a snicker. An uneasiness clouded Lane's heart as they rang off. Placing the receiver securely in its cradle, Root whooped, "There is a God!"

Sticking his head through the Interrogation Room door, Spiegel peered at Root and asked, "What's wrong with you?"

Root wagged his finger, beckoning his partner to step over to book-in. Spiegel sighed and came across the hall. With a wide-faced grin, Root looked around, put his mouth close to Spiegel's ear and said, "Padgett's son bought it on I-70 this afternoon. This might be what we need to break him."

"I'll bet he bawls like a baby when he finds out," Spiegel said.

"You're on. I say he'll be cold as ice and if he does bawl, it'll be fake." Both men laughed and looked around again.

"We have to be careful, Jim," Spiegel said in a low voice. "If they ever find out I'm the one who killed Darby we'll both fry."

"Shhh, Charlie, shut up!" Root hissed. "The last place we should talk about that is in the jail."

In the squad room, Spiegel called the Ottawa County sheriff to request a fax of the accident report. Back in the Interrogation Room, he threw the report down in front of the beaten and bruised preacher. "Poetic justice! There's your proof. Your son's dead, burnt to a crisp in a car wreck."

"Just like you're gonna be," Root sneered, leaning into David's face.

David blinked dumbly as he stared at the fax. "I don't believe it. This is fake," he finally said.

At the door, the deputy shifted from foot to foot. He was about to violate one of the most serious rules in law enforcement by leaving a prisoner alone in an area where escape was possible.

Root and Spiegel had left to take bathroom breaks and he needed one himself. He looked over and saw them back at book-in engaged in what seemed to be a serious discussion. He eyed the men's room across the hall. The prisoner slumped in his chair, defeated. The deputy cracked open the door. Freshly oiled, the hinges made no sound. He heard snippets of conversation floating down the hallway. One part reached his ears with crystal clarity: "…I'm the one who killed Darby we'll both fry."

The deputy closed the door gently and glanced at David. It didn't appear he had heard the fragmented statement that could very well set him free. Now, for reasons other than his physical discomfort, the officer couldn't wait to get out of that room. For the next half hour he was in anguish, mental and physical.

Struggling desperately to maintain his composure, David continued to deny any involvement in the deaths of the three women. Done with talking, both Root and Spiegel threatened, then delivered, physical violence. Finally, Root growled at the deputy, "Get him back to his cell."

"We're not done with you, Padgett," Spiegel barked in David's face as the deputy hauled him off the floor. "Before we're through with you, you'll confess to killing your own mother," Spiegel gathered up the photos while the deputy led David stumbling down the hall. The officer whispered to him, "Don't give up, things are about to change."

Still grappling with his scrambled head, David barely comprehended. A thought crossed his mind—what things?—but he was too confused to ask. Without being aware of it, he was hurried past his isolation cell. Still in a haze, David did not question when the deputy opened the door to cell block E.

The toughest cellblock in the Steuben County Jail, E block was ironically also the most spiritual.

Convicted of murder, Kent Watson was back on appeal after having served 11 years of his sentence at Wabash Valley Correctional Facility in Carlisle, Indiana. Kent's life changed eight years before when another inmate shared Christ with him. Now he and fellow inmate Joshua Ellings served as the prison chaplains' clerks. Together with the chaplains, they brought the light of God into the prisoners' dark world.

David came through the door in the middle of a Bible study Kent was conducting. A dozen or so men seated around a steel picnic table nodded their heads in silent greeting. David's heart cried out for comfort from any quarter. Standing unsteadily at the edge of their circle, he listened to the offender preach.

"There are a lot of deceivers in this world," Kent said, looking slowly from one man to the next and gazing intently into each one's face. "But the greatest one, the father of all lies, is the devil." Some of the men nodded, others did not react. "That old devil, he'll take your life and destroy it any way he can. He'll use drugs, alcohol, money, women, or all of the above."

Later, David discovered the only empty bunk in E block was in Kent's cell.

After dashing to the restroom, the officer checked the hallway to make sure he was alone, then ducked into a stall. His heart racing, he flipped open his cell phone. The number rang once, twice, three times. He was about to close it when someone answered. He faced the wall and whispered into the phone. The restroom door opened. "Who are you sneaking into the bathroom to call?" Root demanded as he pushed open the stall door. The deputy quickly closed the phone and shoved it into his pocket.

"Just... my girlfriend."

"Girlfriend?" Root said, raising his eyebrows and grinning. "I thought you was married."

The young officer looked at him stupidly. "Yeah, yeah, I am."

"Well," Root said, finally moving back from the doorway, "so much for all the muck you're always spouting about a happy marriage. Don't worry, it'll just be between us." He winked at the younger man.

"Thanks," Pete said, edging past the detective.

"Say, Pete." The officer's hand froze on the doorknob. He turned to face Root. "We don't need to say anything to the chief about our little talk with Padgett, okay?"

"Sure," Pete said, making a zipping motion across his lips. Exiting the restroom, the young officer fairly ran from the building.

In E block, Kent was getting acquainted with his new cellmate. After a few minutes he said, "Doc, you say you're saved. Do you believe the Bible is truly the word of God?"

David hesitated. He did once. "Yes, at least certain parts of it."

"Doc, you got to believe all or none of this old book," Kent said, holding up his Bible with one hand and patting its side with the other. "Let me show you something, cuz I read somewhere you've been a-messin' with demons."

Shocked, David protested. "What? No, of course not!"

"You been talking to dead people, ain't that right? Here, read this," Kent turned the Bible around and held it out to David.

David read aloud. "But ye are a chosen generation, a royal priesthood, an holy nation, a peculiar people; that ye should shew forth the praises of Him who hath called you out of darkness into His marvelous light." David reflected on the verse as a light began to shine in his heart.

"Doc, you need to come out of that dark room. You got to quit messin' with the dead and give your life to the living God."

Returning to the squad room, Root settled back in his chair, hoisted his feet onto the desk and closed his eyes. Spiegel came in and poured himself a cup of coffee. Turning too quickly, he dropped the cup, spilling the hot liquid on Root's shoes and causing the detective to jerk and splay his arms.

"Don't make me shoot you, Charlie," Don Price shouted as he charged through the door with his gun drawn. Root lurched forward, his feet hitting the floor. Swinging in Root's direction, Don pointed the pistol at him. "You too, Jim."

Seeing the opportunity, Spiegel drew his .38 from his shoulder holster. He was bringing it up when Don shot him in the right shoulder. He stumbled back, hitting the wall and sliding to the floor with his hand over the bloody hole. Instantly, the room was filled with men in blue or brown uniforms. Don turned to the young officer beside him.

"Pete, since you broke this case, I'm going to give you the privilege of reading the suspects their rights."

Tibb Russell came into his office the next morning on top of the world. Soon Grace Tabernacle would be his new headquarters. He settled at his desk and let out a gleeful little "Hehee!" He'd have a new office overlooking his vast kingdom. First thing to do was rid the place of all that Christian garbage. The door to his office opened. Tibb gasped and clutched his chest. A pain shot through his heart.

176

"Don't die yet, Tibb," David said calmly, "not until you've been tried and convicted for Linda Darby's murder." .

"You... you're crazy, Padgett, we all know who killed her," Tibb sputtered. "Ellen Ridgeway's ring was found under the stove in Linda's house. Your fingerprints were on the knife handle."

"Firsthand knowledge, Tibb? The police never revealed where in the house the ring was discovered."

Slowly, Tibb slid open the middle desk drawer. His fingers closed on the .25 caliber automatic.

"Hands on the desk, Tibb," Don said, stepping through the door followed by five police officers.

"Chief, I'm glad you're here. This murderer was about to rob me."

"The only murderer in this room is you, Russell."

"Don't be absurd." Tibb said, sweat forming on his forehead. "I never killed anyone. You have nothing on me."

Don grinned. "No? Root and Spiegel are singing like a couple of canaries."

Tibb's face went deathly white. Before anyone could stop him, he raised the pistol and shot himself in the head. Rushing to his side, David held him as he died.

"Fooled you, Padgett, I..."

The next day, Don, David, Anne, Lane and Betty sat around the table in the Listons' kitchen. ' Why was Tibb so desperate? He's a billionaire," Anne wondered aloud as she sipped her coffee.

"Was," Don corrected. "His drive to gain more wealth made him greedy. His policies weren't worth the paper they were printed on. He spent people's premiums on the state lottery, then horse racing, and finally in the casinos where he lost all but a few hundred thousand dollars."

"I thought he was my friend," David said. "I believed he really wanted to help me achieve my dream."

"David, in the beginning he did," Don said, "but money was his god."

"A god with feet of clay," Lane said. Everyone nodded.

"Why didn't we know about the confession of the killer at Taylor?" David asked. "He's been in prison for murdering another student for twenty years."

"The DA didn't take it seriously until I insisted on a DNA test," Don said, smiling "So now you're cleared of all charges."

"Thank God for that," David sighed.

"Amen," the others echoed.

Later that night in the prophet's chamber, David lifted his head. The clock on the nightstand read 2:10. Unable to sleep, he prayed, grieving for his son, May, and Ellen. Moonlight streamed through the open window. Outside, crickets chirped and a cow called to her calf. Careful not to wake Anne, David slipped out of bed, dressed and quietly closed the door behind him.

He walked down the hall to a room doubling as the church library and Sunday school room. Selecting a book from the small collection, he read of Moody, Spurgeon and other heroes of the faith. Sitting down at the old typewriter, he wrote the mandate that would govern the rest of his life.

**This day I have come out of darkness into God's marvelous light.**
**I will say with Isaiah, Here am I Lord, send me.**
**As did our Christian forefathers, I will fight the forces of evil.**
**I will do what the Lord asks of me.**
**I will go where He commands.**
**I will love the lost, comfort the dying.**
**I will bring sinners to Christ's salvation.**
**I will give myself unreservedly to His service.**

As he returned to bed, Anne rolled over into his arms. "I love you," she murmured against his chest.

"Oh Anne, sweet Anne, how could I have been so blind?" David asked with tears in his eyes. "I love you so deeply. The Lord and you are my life."

In the darkness, Anne smiled. "I never stopped loving you," she said, kissing him.

"Let's try to get some sleep. Tomorrow, today, is a new day to serve our Lord." Within a few moments, the preacher and his wife nodded off in each other's arms, their sleep sweet and dreamless.

In heaven, Robert, May and Ellen knelt before the Lord. Cradled in her father's arms, Precious smiled as Christ touched Robert's face, wiping the tears from his eyes forever.

# Epilogue

From his office, David looked out at the eight-foot chain link fence, or what was left of it, surrounding the Grace Tabernacle property. Since early this morning, workmen had been busy dismantling it. Already children and families from the neighborhood were fishing in the lake, setting up picnics or simply strolling the paths.

A memorial fund in Robert's name gave hope to needy students. On the mall, The Gap was replaced with a free clothing store for the less fortunate. Free gospel concerts were held in the amphitheater on Saturday nights; in the winter they were performed in the sanctuary. The Upper Room now provided meals for the destitute. Last month the jewelry store and McDonald's were cleared out, the walls between them torn down and a 50-bed dormitory built to shelter the homeless.

The Beautiful You now provided basic hair grooming services to low-income families. A large portrait of Ellen Ridgeway hung on the back wall over a brass plate memorializing her dedication and service to the Lord. The bookstore became a free lending library.

David's books still sold, yet nothing like in the past. The TV and radio programs continued with an entirely different message from the pastor.

With David's help, Kent Watson was paroled and went on to head up a statewide prison and jail ministry for Grace Tabernacle. As a result of the investigation into Tibb Russell's illegal activities, the insurance commission seized what was left of his holdings and refunded pennies on the dollar to his policyholders. Also, the City Council president and two of its members were charged with taking bribes.

The church sold the mansions. David and Anne now live comfortably in a three-bedroom ranch style home. When David travels, Anne goes with him, and today he preaches anywhere for love offerings. The smaller churches call, the larger corporations do not. It took Jenny, the receptionist, some time to accept and become comfortable with the new policy. Of course, receiving Christ into her life helped.

The police found a petition among Russell's effects demanding that David be retained as pastor and signed by over 5,000 persons. As he had for Elijah, God had reserved those faithful ones for himself.

David's office door opened. Anne stepped in, smiling. "Darling, isn't it wonderful?"

He stood and took her in a loving embrace. "Yes," he said, kissing her. "This is the Lord's doing, and it's marvelous in His eyes."

Grasping his hand, Anne said, "Come on, dear, I want to show you something. A robin built a nest in the Redbud tree." Hand-in-hand they walked out into the sunshine.

And so, as the church has for centuries, Grace Tabernacle labors to bring the lost and dying world out of darkness into God's marvelous light.

## The End

**Enjoy Out of Darkness?**

**Keep reading for an excerpt**

**Of  my next novel**

**Never Ending Spring**

**A killer is stalking Elm Grove, Indiana
and the body count is rising.**

# Never Ending Spring

## Prologue

### May 17, 1959

Pulling the patrol car off Mill Creek Road into the weed-infested driveway Sheriff Bob Curry said a silent prayer. "Lord, they don't need this right now; you know the Browns have enough trouble." He sighed and switched off the engine.

Someone was watching, the curtains moved at the front window. Normally such action would make him wary, not today. The Browns were harmless. He hated death notices especially this one. He felt like it was his fault that their son Dennis was dead. He was the one who suggested old man Miller press charges.

"You know sheriff that fence ain't worth much. A little paint might do it some good." Miller said

"Well, with the words the young scalawag put on there its goina have to be painted." Curry said wagging his head. "Tell you what ,I know the Browns can't afford the paint, I'll see if the county can spring for it and we'll let Dennis cool his heels in jail for a couple of days while he paints your fence."

So the deal was struck, now Dennis was dead.

The front door opened and Katy Brown stepped out onto the rickety porch. She clutched her threadbare robe to herself with one hand and holding onto the pealing railing with the other. Her mother eyes searched the interior of the car. Opening the door, Curry walked across the unmowed lawn.

"Morning Mrs. Brown." Bob said squinting up at the gray haired woman.

"Where's Denny, I thought you said he finished the fence yesterday?"

"Well, yes mam he did."

"Then why ain't he with ye, you said you'd bring him by in time for school and its nigh onto 10 o'clock."

"I'm sorry Mrs. Brown; I got some bad news for you. Can I come and talk to you and Don?"

"Now, Sheriff you know wells I do that fight wasn't Denny's fault. Them big boys at the jail gloated him into takin' the first swing. You ain't gonna hold him because of that are ye?" She stood to the side to let him enter. Taking off his hat, Bob ducted his head and stepped into the shabby living room. Don Brown set on the couch his face lined with pain.

"How's the back this morning Don?" Bob ask.

"Not good, I didn't get much sleep last night with it a painin' me."

Taking a deep breath Curry said. "Well folks there's no easy way to say it, Dennis hung himself last night. The night man found him about 5 o'clock this morning. We tried to bring him back, but it was too late"

"NO, NO, NO." Katy Brown screamed." Not my baby. No." She collapsed on the couch tears streaming down her cheeks.

She glared up at the Sheriff. "Denny wouldn't do that. Somebody murdered my little boy."

She said her face lined with anger and sorrow.

Don raised his cane and pointed it shakily at the sheriff.
"You mark my words, somebody killed my son. If'n I was
half the man I used to be I'd be down at that jail and I'd find
out who they is."

They laid Denny out in the living room, in a pine box built
by his uncle Raymond. Uncomfortable going to the home
again Bob waited on the road while they loaded the casket into
their old station wagon. When they pulled out of the yard, he
turned on the bubble and led the small procession down the
mile and a half to the little cemetery, where his granddaddy
and grandma lay.

After they put Denny in the ground, Raymond came to him.
They had known each other for a long time. Curry on one side
of the law Raymond on the other. As much as he tried, Jimmy
could not overcome the alcohol.

"What are you doing here sheriff?" Raymond said bringing
his face inches from Bob's. The smell of cheap beer was
overpowering.

"I came to pay my respects."

"If'n you had respect Denny he wouldn't be in that box."
Raymond took a step closer, his nose almost touching the
sheriff's face.

"Go home Raymond, I don't want to have to arrest you
today." Turning Bob opened the door to his car.

"This aint over sheriff, no sir, this aint over by a long shot."

Raymond stared after the patrol car until it disappeared over
the hill.

Dear Reader:

Writing a novel is somewhat like having a baby. First, there is the thought, then the thought turns into an idea. The idea incubates. Then a story begins to form.

Soon the tale begins to take shape in the writer's mind; the novelist breathes life into the characters. If the writer fashions lifelike characters soon they will began to tell the yarn. The author feels movement. Now it not just a story, but a novel. The process seems long and arduous.

As he or she gets closer to the end the novel's birth, pangs increase. The day of birth-publication-you call friends and family and rejoice together that now your dream is a reality.

Then you dress your dream up in the best cover-after all people still judge a book by its cover-you send it out into the world to succeed or fail. And like a child grown to adulthood you can do little to change your novel after publication. Therefore, I send this novel out for your pleasure. May you enjoy reading Out of Darkness as much as I did writing it.

# More from Darrell Case

The D C Killer is hiding… in the White House. Jerold Robbins is handsome, rich President of the United States and a Serial Killer. Eighteen women have been found floating in the Potomac. Their bodies slashed and weighted down with concrete blocks.

Enjoying the life God intended for you to live
How to enjoy life in spite of yourself.
"

A mmurderer is loose in Elm Grove, Indiana
"Never Ending Spring" is a suspenseful, well-written story."
"Great story about redemption and faith with lots of twists and turns."

Max develops into a serial killer of children. For eighteen years, he operates undetected burying their bodies where they are never found.
"This is a psychological thriller with a wonderful twist. While we get a vivid picture of the psychological character of the killer; we get an even better look at the spiritual fight that goes on around us all the time."

Together Adam and Victoria face a life of ministering, love and danger.

"I loved this book. I could hardly put it down. It is a story of suspense, drama, romance, faith, the love of Jesus as well as of the power of the Holy Spirit and redemption."

"Miracle at Coffeeville is a wonderful collection of Christmas short stories that are very uplifting. It will become a tradition to read this book every year at Christmas If you need something to lift your spirits and put you in the mood for Christmas, grab this book and a cup of hot cocoa, and snuggle in for a heartwarming read."

## ABOUT THE AUTHOR

Darrell Case is the author of several books. He and his wife Connie live in central Indiana.

For news on Darrell's latest books excerpts and actives visit http://darrellcase.com

www.ingramcontent.com/pod-product-compliance
Lightning Source LLC
Chambersburg PA
CBHW031316120626
46554CB00001BA/430